Who Is Israel? Who Is the Church?

PROPHETIC DESTINIES

Who Is Israel? Who Is the Church?

PROPHETIC DESTINIES

DEREK PRINCE

CREATION
HOUSE

BOOKS ABOUT SPIRIT-LED LIVING
LAKE MARY, FLORIDA

Creation House
Strang Communications Company
190 North Westmonte Drive
Altamonte Springs, FL 32714
(407) 862-7565

CONTENTS

INTRODUCTION

One unique feature of the Bible is its predictive prophecies. No sacred book of any other world religion offers anything comparable to the Bible in this respect. Its prophets consistently predicted events of history — with amazing accuracy and descriptive detail — many centuries before they took place. This is one major testimony to the supernatural inspiration of the Bible.

In Isaiah 46:9-10 (NIV) the God of the Bible says of Himself:

> I am God, and there is no other;
> I am God, and there is none like me.
> I make known the end from the beginning,
> From ancient times, what is still to come.
> I say: My purpose will stand,
> And I will do all that I please.

The ability to predict history with such accuracy necessarily implies the ability to control history. For this reason God can say with absolute confidence: "My purpose will stand."

One of the major themes of biblical prophecy is the destiny of Israel. From the birth of Israel as a nation to the final consummation of her destiny, every major stage has been predicted by her own prophets. At least 80 percent of all these prophecies have already been accurately fulfilled. It is therefore altogether reasonable to expect that the remaining 20 percent will be fulfilled with equal accuracy.

Interwoven with the history of Israel is the destiny of another people: the church of Jesus Christ. The church had its origin within Israel, but over the centuries the destinies of these two groups have diverged widely. Yet there has been continuous interaction between them.

The church, too, like Israel, had its prophets. The greatest of these was its founder and reigning head, Jesus of Nazareth. Through Jesus and His apostles, the main outlines of church history were prophetically unfolded in advance. These, too, are being progressively fulfilled.

One vital function of prophecy is to provide God's people with a clear vision of their divinely appointed destiny. Without such a vision they will inevitably stumble and fall. This applies equally to Israel and the church. This is why Solomon says in Proverbs 29:18 that people will perish without a prophetic vision.

The lack of such a vision brought about the downfall of Jerusalem in 586 B.C. After the city had been totally destroyed by the armies of Babylon, the prophet Jeremiah said of her:

> She did not consider her destiny; *therefore* her collapse was awesome (Lam. 1:9, italics added).

About six hundred years later, Jesus Himself spoke in similar terms to the same city:

> If you had known, even you, especially in this your day, the things that make for your peace! But now they are hidden from your eyes. For days will come upon you when your enemies will build an embankment around you, surround you and close you in on every side, and level you, and your children within you, to the ground; and they will not leave in you one stone upon another, because you did not know the time of your visitation (Luke 19:42-44).

Jerusalem, however, is but one outstanding historical example of the tragic consequences that follow when God's people fail to understand their destiny. The same principles apply both to Israel as a people and to the church. In each of these groups, failure to understand their destiny will result in tragedy.

But this need not happen! Through the prophetic Scriptures, God has provided — for Israel and the church — all they need to understand and fulfill their destiny. May it not be said of one or the other that failure and disaster came "because you did not know the time of your visitation."

One of the most exciting features of the period in which we live is that the destinies of Israel and the church are once again converging. Their convergence will produce the most dramatic and significant developments of all human history.

My own contact with Jerusalem and the land of Israel goes back to the year 1942, while I was serving with the British Forces in the Middle East. In the fifty years that have passed since then, I have witnessed the fulfillment of many significant biblical prophecies. In 1948 I was an eyewitness to the events that climaxed in the birth of the state of Israel, and I have continued to follow the subsequent development of the state. I currently reside in Jerusalem.

The progressive fulfillment of biblical prophecy during this whole period has had the effect of focusing the attention of both Jews and Christians on one future event of unique importance to both: the coming of the Messiah.

My sincere desire and prayer are that this book will give a clearly outlined picture of the awesome developments which lie ahead, both for Israel and for the church.

Derek Prince
Jerusalem, Israel
1992

CHAPTER ONE

THE DESTINY OF ISRAEL AND THE CHURCH

The Focus of World Attention

Why is Israel the focus of attention in the world's media? Why do pragmatic and statesmanlike world leaders erupt with emotional outbursts when Israel is discussed? Why does the United Nations devote 30 percent of its time and one-third of its resolutions to Israel — a tiny country with a population of only five million?

There is only one source for a clear and authoritative answer: the Bible. Although it was completely written almost two thousand years before the current problems in the Middle East arose, the Bible provides a supernaturally inspired analysis of both the issues and the forces that are involved.

Israel occupies a unique place in the current controversies, because the place which Israel occupies in God's purposes is likewise unique. God's prophetic Word reveals that this present age will culminate with the restoration and redemption of Israel. The nearer we come to the close of the age, therefore, the more intense will be the pressures surrounding Israel.

These events that center around Israel will also determine the destiny of Satan, the age-old adversary of God and man. In 2 Corinthians 4:4 Satan is called "the god of this age." He is well aware that when Israel's redemption is completed and this age closes, he will no longer be able to pose as a god. He will be stripped of his power to deceive and manipulate humanity and will be subject to the judgment of God. Consequently, he is at this time deploying all his deceptive strategy and exercising all his evil power to resist the process that will lead to Israel's restoration and ultimate redemption.

Here, then, are the two main spiritual forces that meet in conflict over the Middle East: on the one hand, the grace of God working toward Israel's restoration; and on the other hand, the deceitful strategies of Satan, who is opposing this process by every means in his power. This is the real but invisible reason for the struggles and tensions which Israel is currently experiencing.

A major part of Satan's strategy against Israel has been to obscure the truth as revealed in the Bible. It is amazing that so much confusion has existed, and still exists, in the church today concerning God's purposes for Israel. The battle for Israel is, in fact, the battle for truth. There are two vital areas of truth which we will consider in this book: Israel's identity and Israel's destiny. After we have examined these, we must consider whether the destiny of Israel also sheds light on the destiny of the church. Finally, we will discuss the responsibility of the church toward Israel in this hour of crisis.

Who Is Israel?

Almost limitless misunderstanding, ignorance and distortion have pervaded the church for many centuries concerning the identity of Israel. This seems extraordinary to me because the statements in the Bible regarding Israel are so clear. Nevertheless, the minds of multitudes of Christians seem to be clouded in regard to the application of the name *Israel*.

In a later section of this book we will consider a parallel topic: the way the word *church* is used in the New Testament (see chapter 3). There, too, we shall discover that the identity of the true church, like that of Israel, has been clouded in a confusion that obscures the real purposes of God.

The origin of the confusion concerning Israel may be traced back to the early church fathers, who developed a doctrine that the church had replaced Israel in the purposes of God and was to be known as the "new Israel." This kind of teaching was promulgated about 150 A.D. by Justin Martyr and was later adopted and amplified by such celebrated figures as Irenaeus, Origen and Augustine. More and more, the Old Testament was interpreted in an "allegorical" way, which no longer did justice to the plain meaning of many texts.

Significantly, at about the same period the doc-

13

trine of the church as a whole was being progressively corrupted from the purity and simplicity of the apostolic revelation contained in the New Testament. The eventual outcome of this process was the church of the Dark Ages, which was, for the most part, spiritually, morally and doctrinally corrupt.

From about 400 A.D., Israel has regularly been used by Bible teachers, commentators and even translators as a synonym for the church. For instance, a certain edition of the King James Version (from which I preached for thirty-five years) has the following headings at the top of the pages in the latter chapters of Isaiah:

Chapter 43 opens with the words, "But now thus saith the Lord that created thee, O Jacob, and he that formed thee, O Israel, Fear not...." But the heading at the top of the page reads, "God comforteth *the church* with his promises" (italics added).

Again, chapter 44 opens with the words, "Yet now hear, O Jacob my servant; and Israel, whom I have chosen...." But the heading at the top of the page reads, *"The church* comforted" (italics added).

Headings such as these, inserted in the text, produce an effect that is subliminal — that is, below the threshold of conscious awareness. Nevertheless, their cumulative impact over the centuries is beyond our power to calculate. Many generations of Christians have unconsciously assumed that the headings are part of the original text. But they are not! Supplied by editors many centuries later, they misrepresent what Isaiah is actually saying, applying to the church words that are specifically addressed by name to Israel.

Essential truth is usually simple. And the truth is, Israel is Israel, and the church is the church.

To recover the truth about the identity of Israel it is necessary to go back to the actual text of the New Testament and see how the apostles used the term *Israel*. This is the only legitimate basis for a scripturally accurate use of this term. Ever since the canon of Scripture was closed, no subsequent writer or preacher has been authorized to change the usage established by the apostolic writers of the New Testament. Any writer or preacher who introduces a different application of the term *Israel* forfeits the right to claim scriptural authority for what he or she has to say about Israel.

I have discovered seventy-nine instances in the New Testament where the words *Israel* or *Israelite* occur.* After examining them all, I conclude that the apostles never used Israel as a synonym for the church.

Nor does the phrase *the new Israel* occur anywhere in the New Testament. Preachers who use that phrase should take care to define their use of it. They should also state that it is not found in the Bible.

Some years ago, while I was addressing a group in Israel, I happened to remark that Israel is never used in Scripture as a synonym for the church. The people in the group were mature believers, dedicated to seeing God's plan for the Jewish people fulfilled. Yet one of them — a long-

---

* The reader would do well to read carefully through the complete list given in Appendix A.

time friend — told me afterward, "That's the first time I have ever heard anyone say that Israel is not a synonym for the church." This remark helped me to see how widespread this misinterpretation is.

Israel is, on the other hand, often used as a type of the church. Concerning the experiences of Israel in the Exodus, Paul says:

> Now all these things happened to them as examples [or types], and they were written for our admonition (1 Cor. 10:11).

To portray Israel as a type of the church, however, is altogether different from identifying the church as Israel.

Consider, by way of illustration, that Jomo Kenyatta, the first president of Kenya, could be described as "the George Washington of his people" in the same way that George Washington is considered the national father of the United States. In other words, much that applies to George Washington in regard to the United States applies to Jomo Kenyatta in regard to Kenya. But this is not to say that Jomo Kenyatta actually *was* George Washington. It is just as incorrect to say that the church *is* Israel.

Unfortunately, the church has been strongly influenced by a "Christian" principle of interpretation that is seldom stated explicitly: All the blessings apply to the church, and all the curses apply to Israel. Behind this principle of interpretation lies the assertion (in which there is much truth) that Israel had her chance but was unfaithful to God. This line of reasoning continues with the belief that God has changed His mind and reapplied His promises, once reserved for Israel, to the church. Such a conclusion, however, clearly impugns the faithfulness of God.

Paul expresses his reaction to such a suggestion in Romans 3:3-4. Analyzing the consequences of Israel's unfaithfulness, he says:

> For what if some did not believe? Will their unbelief make the faithfulness of God without effect? Certainly not! Indeed, let God be true but every man a liar.

As previously stated, the only legitimate way to ascertain the correct use of words such as *Jew* or *Israel* is to examine the actual passages in the New Testament where they occur.

Who Is a Jew?

To begin with, let us look at the word *Jew*, which occurs in the New Testament nearly two hundred times. Out of all these occurrences, the only passage in which *Jew* is clearly used in a way different from the accepted norm is Romans 2:28-29.

These verses come at the end of a chapter in which Paul has been explaining — with particular reference to the Jewish people — that knowledge of God's will through the law justifies no one. A person is not righteous simply because he knows what is right. On the contrary, Paul says, that knowledge merely increases human responsibility. He goes on to apply this specifically to the Jewish people of his day.

Before using this statement against the Jewish people today, however, we need to bear in mind that nineteen centuries have elapsed. In Paul's day it was primarily the Jewish people who had the knowledge of God. Today it is we Christians who claim to have the full knowledge of the revealed will of God, because we believe the whole Bible. Paul's warning to the Jews of his day is probably needed equally by the church of our day. The fact that we know the will of God and what is right does not make us righteous. On the contrary, it only increases our responsibility.

After pointing out that the Jews of his day had in many cases fallen short of God's will and substituted a legalistic form of religion for the real purpose of God in the Scriptures, Paul closes the chapter with these words:

> For he is not a Jew who is one outwardly, nor is circumcision that which is outward in the flesh; but he is a Jew who is one inwardly; and circumcision is that of the heart, in the Spirit, not in the letter; whose praise is not from men but from God (Rom. 2:28-29).

When Paul says "whose praise is not from men," he is playing on the Hebrew meaning of the name *Jew*, which is taken from the name of the tribe of Judah, meaning "praise" or "thanksgiving." When Leah gave birth to her fourth son she called him Judah (in Hebrew, *Yehuda*), saying, "I will praise the Lord." The meaning of Judah (*Ye-*

huda) or *Jew*, then, is "praise." So Paul says if you are a real Jew, your praise should come from God and not from men. In a certain sense, he is restricting the use of the word *Jew* here. He is saying that it is not enough to be a Jew outwardly. A true Jew, in addition to being a Jew by birth, or conversion, must have the inner condition of heart that earns him or her the praise of God. It is important to understand here that Paul is not extending the use of the term *Jew*. On the contrary, he is restricting it.

Some years ago I read an article in a British magazine in which the writer heaped criticism upon Israel and derived from this passage in Romans the theory that we are all Jews! That is far out of line with the teaching of the New Testament. It must surely confuse Jewish people to be told that when we are in Christ, "there is neither Jew nor Gentile," only to hear later, "But we are all Jews."

Nor is that what Paul is contemplating. He is saying that to be a real Jew it is not enough that a person have all the outward marks. He or she must also have the inward spiritual condition that gives praise to God and earns praise from Him.

Put the same idea in a Christian context. We might say to someone, If you are a real Christian, when somebody strikes you on one cheek you will turn the other. But we would not mean to imply that those who do not turn the other cheek are not entitled to be called Christians. The special use of *Christian* in this context obviously would not replace the normal, accepted use of the word.

In addition to Romans 2, there are two passages — Revelation 2:9 and 3:9 — where the Lord speaks of "those who say they are Jews and are not." There are various possible ways to interpret these passages. They could possibly refer to the same kind of people Paul describes in Romans 2 — those who have the outward marks of being Jewish but lack the inward spiritual requirement.

Suppose, however, we accept these two passages in Revelation, together with that in Romans, as examples of a special use of the term *Jew*, which restricts the term to Jews who fulfill certain spiritual requirements. The fact remains that out of nearly two hundred passages in the New Testament, there are only three examples in which *Jew* refers to the restricted meaning. In those three examples, *Jews* refers to those who are related to God through faith in the Messiah. To interpret a verse using this restricted meaning of the word, it must be clearly required by the context. The extended application of the term *Jew* (that Jews are all those who are rightly related to God through Jesus Christ) is not found in the New Testament and could never replace the normal meaning of the word *Jew*.

CHAPTER TWO

"THEY ARE NOT ISRAEL"

Now we will turn to the words *Israel* and *Israelites* as used in the New Testament. I have counted seventy-nine passages where these words occur in the New Testament (see a complete list in Appendix A). In nine cases these are direct quotations of Old Testament Scripture verses, and in every instance the meaning in the New Testament is precisely the same as in the Old. There are sixty-eight passages beyond that which are not quotations from the Old Testament, but in all these cases the use in the New Testament agrees with that of the Old.

There remain, therefore, only two passages in the New Testament where *Israel* is used with a special sense. As with the word *Jew*, this special New Testament usage of *Israel* does not extend but restricts the application of the word.

The first such restricted use is found in Romans 9:6-9, where Paul explains that even though Israel did not in many instances receive or obey the word of God, this does not mean the word of God had no effect:

> For they are not all Israel who are of Israel, nor are they all children because they are the seed of Abraham; but, "In Isaac your seed shall be called." That is, those who are the children of the flesh, these are not the children of God; but the children of the promise are counted as the seed. For this is the word of promise: "At this time I will come and Sarah shall have a son."

Paul explains here that to be physically descended from Israel — that is, from Jacob — is not sufficient. To qualify for God's promised blessing, a person must also demonstrate the same faith that characterized Abraham, Isaac and Jacob, otherwise he or she is not really entitled to the name *Israel*.

Let me emphasize once again that Paul is not extending the use of *Israel* to include all believers, irrespective of national origin. On the contrary, he is restricting its use to include only those descendants of Israel who are in the faith of the Messiah. It is in error to suggest that in this passage Paul uses the word *Israel* to describe all believers.

In other places in Romans 9, Paul uses *Israel* in the normal sense of all who are descended from Abraham, Isaac and Jacob. In verses 3-5, for instance, he says:

For I could wish that I myself were accursed from Christ for my brethren, my countrymen according to the flesh, who are *Israelites*, to whom pertain the adoption, the glory, the covenants, the giving of the law, the service of God, and the promises; of whom are the fathers and from whom, according to the flesh, Christ came, who is over all, the eternally blessed God. Amen (italics added).

Here Paul identifies as Israelites those who have actually rejected the Messiah. Nevertheless he calls them his countrymen. "I could wish that I myself were accursed from Christ for [them]," he writes. In other words, Paul wishes he could take their place of unbelief and rejection by God. Paul is obviously using the name *Israel* or *Israelites* here to describe all those descended from Abraham, Isaac and Jacob, whether they are believers or unbelievers. This is the normal use throughout the New Testament.

The Israel of God

The other passage in which Paul uses *Israel* in a restricted sense is Galatians 6:15-16:

For in Christ Jesus neither circumcision nor uncircumcision avails anything, but a new creation. And as many as walk according to this rule, peace and mercy be upon them, and upon the Israel of God.

23

Paul is talking about two kinds of people. On the one hand are those who, without a background in circumcision or Judaism, have experienced the new birth and are walking in the new creation. On the other hand are Israelites by natural descent who have remained in the faith that was the mark of their ancestors and through that faith have embraced Jesus as Messiah, thus entering into the new covenant. Paul calls this group of people "the Israel of God." What really matters, Paul is saying, is not some religious rite but a creative act of God in the heart generated by the new covenant.

It is interesting, however, that the New International Version, one of the most widely used modern versions, departs from normal translation principles at this point. Verse 16 in that version reads: "Peace and mercy to all who follow this rule, *even* to the Israel of God" (italics added). *Even* has been substituted for the normal *and*. Meaning what? That those who walk according to this rule are "the Israel of God," whether they are Jews or Gentiles.

This substitution is based not on linguistic grounds but on theological grounds. The Greek word is *kai*. You would have to search the New Testament to find places where that word is legitimately translated "even" — probably fewer than once in five hundred occurrences. Overwhelmingly *kai* is translated "and." What prompted the NIV translators to change *and* to *even* on this occasion? Apparently the old tradition that all true believers are the "Israel of God." This thinking has so influenced Christians that they will change the plain meaning of a text to bring it in line with their theology!

This is not an attack on the NIV translators, who on the whole have produced an excellent version. It serves merely to illustrate the extent to which this "spiritual Israel" theory has penetrated the thinking of the church, producing attitudes and forms of thought which have no solid basis in the Scriptures.

There is an important reason why Paul makes a distinction in Galatians 6:15-16 between believers from Gentile and Jewish backgrounds. Gentiles, on the one hand, had become Christians by a single supernatural transformation that had taken place in their hearts. They had no previous background of knowledge of the one true God. For Jews, on the other hand, their faith in the Messiah was the culmination of a historical process which was initiated at the exodus from Egypt and then developed over many centuries through the ministry of God-appointed rulers, prophets and priests.

The spiritual condition of the Gentile world at the time of the writing of the New Testament could be compared to a field which had been left in its natural wild condition, never having been cultivated. A Gentile's conversion to Christ represented a direct intervention of God in one whose heart had not been prepared by a Jewish heritage.

The Jewish people, on the other hand, were a field that had been carefully cultivated over many centuries. For this reason, during the period of His ministry that was confined to Israel, Jesus said to His disciples: "I sent you to reap that for which you have not labored; others have labored, and you have entered into their labors" (John 4:38). The disciples were reaping in a field that had been cultivated over many centuries by a long succession of God's servants.

The terminology that Paul uses in Galatians 6:15-16 brings out this distinction between the backgrounds of Gentile and Jewish believers. For both there was a personal encounter with the Messiah, which transformed their lives. For Gentiles this was a direct intervention of God, without any historical process of preparation. But for Jews the encounter was the culmination of a historical process that had been going on for many centuries. It was appropriate, therefore, to describe them not just as *Israel* but as *the Israel of God*. Their faith in the Messiah represented the fulfillment of the purpose for which God had brought Israel into being.

It must be emphasized, however, that these verses in Galatians do not by any means represent the normal use of *Israel* in the New Testament.

Israel as Distinguished From the Church

We have established that *Israel* is never used in the New Testament as a synonym for the church. On the contrary, the opposite is actually true. In some passages the word *Israel* even denotes Jews who have actually rejected Jesus, and so they cannot possibly be considered as members of His church.

We will look at just a few such passages in Romans 11:

What then? Israel has not obtained what it seeks; but the elect have obtained it, and the rest were blinded (v. 7).

Here *Israel* is obviously used to describe those who have *not* believed in Jesus the Messiah and are therefore not part of the church. In the same chapter Paul says about Israel:

I say then, have they stumbled that they should fall? Certainly not! But through their fall, to provoke them to jealousy, salvation has come to the Gentiles. Now if their fall is riches for the world, and their failure riches for the Gentiles, how much more their fullness! For I speak to you Gentiles; inasmuch as I am an apostle to the Gentiles, I magnify my ministry, if by any means I may provoke to jealousy those who are my flesh and save some of them (vv. 11-14).

Throughout these verses Paul maintains a consistent contrast between Israelites who have rejected Jesus and Gentiles who have received salvation through faith in Him. So, far from Israel being a name *for* Gentile believers, Paul uses the name to distinguish them *from* Gentile believers!

We can also read in Romans 11:

For I do not desire, brethren, that you should be ignorant of this mystery, lest you should be wise in your own opinion, that blindness in part has happened to

Israel until the fullness [full number] of
the Gentiles has come in (v. 25).

The same ignorance that Paul was struggling
against nearly two thousand years ago, the ignorance concerning God's plan for Israel, still persists today. Nevertheless this passage makes it
clear again that Paul sets unbelieving Israelites
in contrast with Gentiles who have become believers. They are not identified in any way with Gentile Christians; rather they are distinguished
from them.

Paul concludes with this wonderful statement
in verse 26: "And so all Israel will be saved." If
Israel were a synonym for the church, with *the
church* being defined as those who are saved, then
the statement in verse 26 would be ridiculous.
Paul would be saying that all those who are saved
will be saved. Such an interpretation must therefore be rejected.

CHAPTER THREE

WHO IS THE CHURCH?

This analysis of the use of *Israel* in the New Testament would not be complete without a similar brief analysis of the way in which the New Testament uses the word *church*. Many people today think of a church as a physical structure of wood or brick or stone, but this is not the New Testament usage of the word.

In the Greek text of the New Testament, the word usually translated "church" is *ekklesia*. This denotes a company of people called out for a special purpose. The closest English word would be *assembly*. In Acts 19:32, 39 and 41, it is the word used to describe the body of citizens in Ephesus who were held collectively accountable for the conduct of affairs in the city.

In like manner, according to the usage in the New Testament, the church is an assembly of people called out from the present world order to serve Jesus Christ and to be prepared by Him to become the collective instrument of the government which He will establish in the next age.

In Ephesians 1:22-23 Paul further describes the church as "His [Christ's] body." Seen in this light, the church is not an organization but an organism. Each member of this body is directly related to all the other members through personal faith in Christ.

Over the centuries, however, this concept has been so corrupted and distorted that the church, as it is known today, bears little or no resemblance to the original model established in the New Testament. Many of those who consider themselves as members of today's church have no living, personal relationship with Christ and are often at enmity with other professing Christians. Consequently, a great many of those who call themselves Christians are not members of this church which the apostle Paul describes.

In the midst of all this confusion, however, the true church is still here on earth. Concerning this Paul says in 2 Timothy 2:19:

> Nevertheless the solid foundation of God stands, having this seal: "The Lord knows those who are His," and, "Let everyone who names the name of Christ depart from iniquity."

The church, so defined, has two distinguishing characteristics. First, God — and God alone — knows all those who are truly His. Second, everyone who claims to be a member of this church is required to demonstrate it by a life of practical righteousness and holiness.

For most Jewish people, this New Testament picture of the church has no reality. They think of the church as a large institution, on the same order as a political party or an ethnic group, which for many centuries has been the main instrument and propagator of anti-Semitism. Thus the confusion produced by Satan concerning the identity of Israel is exceeded only by the confusion he has produced concerning the identity of the church.

Election

Israel and the church, as correctly interpreted, have one vitally important element in common: each of them is the product of what theologians term *divine election*. More simply stated, this means "God's choice."

Much of the controversy concerning Israel revolves around this issue of God's choice. If there is anything the natural mind of unregenerate man does not like, it is the revelation that God has chosen certain people. We can usually tolerate it so long as we believe *we* are the people God has chosen. Our problem comes when God says He has chosen people whom we would *not* have chosen! To the humanist, the truth of divine election is like waving the proverbial red flag before a bull.

In Romans 9:10-18 Paul offers an historical example of election from the Old Testament — the birth of Jacob and Esau. Both twins were conceived by the same father, but before they were born God declared His attitude toward each of them. Paul says God did this to demonstrate that the decisive issue in a person's destiny is not what he does, but what God chooses. This has never been an easy doctrine for the carnal mind of man to receive.

> And not only this, but when Rebecca also had conceived by one man, even by our father Isaac (for the children not yet being born, nor having done any good or evil, that the purpose of God according to election might stand, not of works but of Him who calls), it was said to her, "The older shall serve the younger." As it is written, "Jacob I have loved, but Esau I have hated" (vv. 10-13).

Before these two brothers ever came out of the womb, without reference to anything they had done, God declared His choice. Moreover, having the older serve the younger was contrary to the accepted cultural rules of the day. Clearly God's choice was not based on Jacob's character or good deeds, because he had not even been born. On the other hand, any goodness that subsequently came out of Jacob's life was the fruit of God's choice.

Paul then suggests the way many people probably react upon reading this:

> What shall we say then? Is there unrighteousness with God? Certainly not! For He says to Moses, "I will have mercy on whomever I will have mercy, and I will have compassion on whomever I will have compassion" (vv. 14-15).

Mercy and compassion come from God's sovereign decision. Unfortunately, however, the truth of God's sovereignty is hardly ever mentioned in the contemporary church. We could define God's sovereignty by saying God does what He wants, when He wants to, and the way He wants to do it. He asks no one's permission. (That is what really disturbs the humanists. He doesn't consult them!)

> So then it is not of him who wills, nor of him who runs, but of God who shows mercy (v. 16).

All our effort and all our good works are not sufficient. We are totally dependent on God's mercy, which He Himself freely dispenses as He chooses.

In the following verse Paul quotes from Exodus 9:16, where God speaks of His judgment:

> For the Scripture says to the Pharaoh, "For this very purpose I have raised you up, that I may show My power in you, and that My name may be declared in all the earth" (v. 17).

Pharaoh was a singularly wicked ruler, yet it was God who raised him up. God did this that He might make Pharaoh a demonstration to all succeeding generations of His judgment on rulers who oppose the purpose and the people of God.

Paul concludes this section by emphasizing that it is God who by His own sovereign decision either grants or withholds mercy in the life of every person.

> Therefore He has mercy on whom He wills, and whom He wills He hardens (v. 18).

We always need to remember that God does not owe mercy to any of us. It proceeds solely from His grace. If He never offered mercy to a single one of us, He would still be perfectly just.

When God offers His mercy, He lays down certain simple conditions that He requires us to meet. These are stated in the message of the gospel. The fact that we have met His conditions for mercy, however, by no means indicates that we have earned it. By definition, neither mercy nor grace can ever be earned.

The Elect Remnant

These principles of mercy and judgment apply universally to the whole human race, but in Romans 9 Paul illustrates them by the particular example of God's dealings with Israel. He reveals that those Israelites whom God has actually chosen for Himself will be only a remnant out of all Israel.

It is significant that this word *remnant* is applied to Israel in Scripture more than forty times. In most of these instances the reference is to the period just prior to the close of the present age.

In Romans 9:27 Paul quotes a prophecy from Isaiah 10:22 concerning Israel:

> Though the number of the children of Israel be as the sand of the sea, the remnant will be saved.

The word *the* in front of remnant is significant. It denotes a precise number chosen out of all Israel.

In Romans 11:1-4 Paul returns to this theme of a remnant. In verse 4 he quotes 1 Kings 19:18, referring to the condition of Israel during the period of Elijah's ministry, when God declared, "I have reserved for Myself seven thousand men who have not bowed the knee to Baal." When God says, "I have reserved for Myself...," He emphasizes that these seven thousand were reserved by God on the basis of His grace, not of their good deeds. It was not something they had earned.

Paul goes on to apply these words to the condition of Israel in his day:

> Even so then, at this present time there is a remnant according to the election of grace.... But if it is of works, it is no longer grace; otherwise work is no longer work (Rom. 11:5-6).

Paul explains that grace goes beyond anything that we can earn by good works. In fact, grace begins in our lives precisely where our own ability reaches its limit. So it is with the remnant of Israel. Their preservation is due to God's grace; it is not something they have earned or can earn.

In Romans 11:26 Paul looks forward to a time when "all Israel will be saved." In the light of what he has said previously about a remnant, it becomes clear that the "all Israel" who will be saved will be the remnant whom God has chosen and reserved for Himself by His grace.

Many other passages from the prophets emphasize that those to whom these promises of restoration are given are a remnant. For instance, Zephaniah 3:12-13, which is addressed to Israel and Jerusalem, declares:

> I will leave in your midst
> A meek and humble people,
> And they shall trust in the name of the
> Lord.
> The *remnant* of Israel shall do no un-
> righteousness
> And speak no lies,
> Nor shall a deceitful tongue be found
> in their mouth... (italics added).

God's end purpose in dealing with Israel as a people is to produce that remnant. For their sakes He has patiently endured the appalling wickedness with which, over many centuries, man has persistently violated God's laws and desecrated the earth. He has also permitted the many sorrows and sufferings with which it has been necessary to purify His chosen ones.

At the end of it all, what is God looking for? A meek and humble people who will trust in the name of the Lord.

This is a good example of one way in which Israel is a type for the church. What is God aiming to produce in the church? A meek and humble people who will trust in the Lord.

The same principle is unfolded in Zechariah 13:8-9 (although a question exists as to the historical context):

"And it shall come to pass in all the
    land,"
Says the Lord,
"That two-thirds in it shall be cut off
    and die,
But one-third shall be left in it:
I will bring the one-third through the
    fire,
Will refine them as silver is refined,
And test them as gold is tested.
They will call on My name,
And I will answer them.
I will say, 'This is My people';
And each one will say, 'The Lord is my
    God.' "

Again the Bible is describing the process aimed at producing the remnant God has chosen. Even though it involves refining and testing by fire, God will not cease until His purpose is accomplished. Two-thirds may be cut off, but the remaining one-third will be brought through the fire to acknowledge the Lord personally as their God. This is the remnant God has set His heart on from eternity. They may appropriately be called "the Israel of God."

CHAPTER FOUR

Israel's Past and Future

Israel's Sinfulness

When I was a young preacher, I delighted in pointing out all the faults and inconsistencies of the church. But I came to realize this doesn't help much; it accomplishes little that is positive. Nor does it require cleverness to point out the faults of the church. Anybody can do it.

Likewise, it takes no cleverness to point out the faults of Israel. Somebody showed me a copy of an article recently published in a Christian magazine pointing out some of the sins of Israel. I could not help reflecting that the prophets of Israel did a much more thorough job! How could anyone add to the recital of sins found in Isaiah 1? God Himself declares these sins to all who will hear:

Hear, O heavens, and give ear, O earth!

38

For the Lord has spoken:
"I have nourished and brought up children,
And they have rebelled against Me..."
(v. 2).

The Hebrew emphasizes *they*, meaning that the very ones God nourished and brought up are the ones who have rebelled against Him.

Verses 4-6 picture a nation sick from the crown of its head to the soles of its feet; there is not a single sound place in it.

Alas, sinful nation,
A people laden with iniquity,
A brood of evildoers,
Children who are corrupters!
They have forsaken the Lord,
They have provoked to anger
The Holy One of Israel,
They have turned away backward.
Why should you be stricken again?
You will revolt more and more.
The whole head is sick,
And the whole heart faints.
From the sole of the foot even to the
head,
There is no soundness in it,
But wounds and bruises and putrefy-
ing sores;
They have not been closed or bound up,
Or soothed with ointment (vv. 4-6).

In verses 12-15 the Lord declares that all Is-rael's religious rituals cannot commend them to

Him, but merely provoke His total rejection. He closes with the words:

> Even though you make many prayers,
> I will not hear.
> Your hands are full of blood (v. 15).

The theme of Israel's sinfulness recurs throughout Isaiah. For instance, no modern writer could pen an indictment of them more vivid and severe than the words of Isaiah 59:2-8:

> But your iniquities have separated you
>   from your God;
> And your sins have hidden His face
>   from you,
> So that He will not hear.
> For your hands are defiled with blood,
> And your fingers with iniquity;
> Your lips have spoken lies,
> Your tongue has muttered perversity.
>
> No one calls for justice,
> Nor does any plead for truth.
> They trust in empty words and speak
>   lies;
> They conceive evil and bring forth iniq-
>   uity.
> They hatch vipers' eggs and weave the
>   spider's web;
> He who eats of their eggs dies,
> And from that which is crushed a viper
>   breaks out.
>
> Their webs will not become garments,

Nor will they cover themselves with
   their works;
Their works are works of iniquity,
And the act of violence is in their
   hands.
Their feet run to evil,
And they make haste to shed innocent
   blood;
Their thoughts are thoughts of iniquity;
Wasting and destruction are in their
   paths.
The way of peace they have not known,
And there is no justice in their ways;
They have made themselves crooked
   paths;
Whoever takes that way shall not
   know peace.

Furthermore, similar indictments are found in
most of Israel's other prophets. This is all the
more significant because the same prophets who
described in clear detail the sins of Israel also
predicted with equal clarity and detail the restoration of Israel.

If the prophets of Israel had been blind, senti-
mental and nationalistic and had overlooked the
sins of their people, then we could say that their
promises of restoration were merely unrealistic,
wishful thinking. But because the same prophets
who promised restoration were the ones who uttered the indictments, I see no logic or consis-
tency in endorsing the indictments and refusing
the promises of restoration.

Israel's Restoration Predicted

The prophets of Israel certainly do make clear, specific promises of a restoration of Israel which will take place in two phases: first to their land and then to their God. I always put it in that order because I see in Scripture that God purposes to bring most of the Jews back to the land unredeemed, not in faith, in order that He may deal with them there. This is stated in Hosea 1:10:

> In the place where it was said to them,
> "You are not My people,"
> There it shall be said to them,
> "You are sons of the living God."

The place where God said, "You are not My people," was the land of Israel. Consequently, the Jews' restoration and acceptance by God has to take place in the land of Israel.

There is a practical reason for this which is not readily appreciated in our contemporary, Western version of Christianity. Under the influence of secular values, we have made the Christian faith primarily a matter of a person's individual relationship with his God. Our emphasis is mainly on the word *my* — my Savior, my faith, my church, my ministry and so on. But this does not accurately represent the biblical perspective.

Throughout the Scriptures God deals with individuals in the context of a larger group — a family, a community, a congregation, a nation. This is brought out in the account of the salvation of the Philippian jailer in Acts 16:30-31. The jailer asked the apostles, "What must I do to be saved?"

In his inspired answer, however, Paul went beyond the jailer's individual need: "Believe on the Lord Jesus Christ, and you will be saved, you *and your household*" (italics added). The salvation which the Lord offered extended beyond the jailer as an individual and embraced his whole household. That is the biblical norm. God regularly deals with the individual in the context of a larger entity.

Historically, this has always been true of God's dealings with Israel. He has consistently related to them not just as individuals, but as a single people, joined by a covenant both to God and to one another. This is how God intends to deal with them at the close of this age — as a single people. In order to do this, however, He must gather them once again in one place. The place indicated both by logic and by Scripture is their own land — the land of Israel.

A further promise of spiritual restoration is found in Isaiah 45:17, 25:

> But Israel shall be saved by the Lord
> With an everlasting salvation;
> You shall not be ashamed or disgraced
> Forever and ever.
>
> In the Lord all the descendants of Is-
>   rael
> Shall be justified, and shall glory.

That is so simple! The word *justified* means "acquitted, counted righteous before God." In other words, Israel's righteousness will be imputed to them on the basis of faith, not of works. They will thus become true spiritual descendants of their forefather Abraham, who "believed in the Lord, and He accounted it to him for righteousness" (Gen. 15:6).

How many of the descendants of Israel will be justified in this way? *Every* person who is justified. But bear in mind that these Israelites will only be a remnant (see chapter 8).

Another promise of Israel's restoration is found in Jeremiah 32:36-37:

> Now therefore, thus says the Lord, the God of Israel, concerning this city [Jerusalem] of which you say, "It shall be delivered into the hand of the king of Babylon by the sword, by the famine, and by the pestilence: Behold, I will gather them out of all countries where I have driven them in My anger, in My fury, and in great wrath; I will bring them back to this place [which was the land of Israel], and I will cause them to dwell safely."

This prediction was certainly not fulfilled by the partial and temporary return from Babylon in the time of Zerubbabel. Nor can it be applied in any meaningful way to the church. Yet this passage in Jeremiah 32 is only one of many prophecies that contain the same promise of Israel's ultimate and total restoration.

We are therefore left with only two possible conclusions: Either these predictions are to be fulfilled in the destiny of Israel, or God has uttered prophecies that will never be fulfilled. In the last resort, it is not just the destiny of Israel which is at stake. There is an issue of even greater importance that concerns all believers. It is *the reliability of Scripture itself.*

Israel's Restoration Described

In Jeremiah 32:38-42 God continues:

> "They shall be My people, and I will be their God; then I will give them one heart and one way, that they may fear Me forever, for the good of them and their children after them. And I will make an everlasting covenant with them, that I will not turn away from doing them good; but I will put My fear in their hearts so that they will not depart from Me. Yes, I will rejoice over them to do them good, and I will assuredly plant them in this land, with all My heart and with all My soul." For thus says the Lord: "Just as I have brought all this great calamity on this people, so I will bring on them all the good that I have promised them."

God declares that He will bring upon Israel the good that He has promised to them in just the same way that He brought calamity upon them. The calamity that came upon them was a matter of objective historical fact. It was not merely "metaphorical" or "spiritual." Therefore the good that God will bring upon them will likewise be objective history. It will not be merely "metaphorical" or "spiritual."

The land in which God says He "will assuredly plant" His people can be interpreted in no other way than the land of Israel. And if God does this with all His heart and soul, who can undo it? Surely not a Palestinian leader! Nor even the United Nations!

In Jeremiah 50:19-20 God further unfolds His plan to restore Israel:

> "But I will bring back Israel to his
> home,
> And he shall feed on Carmel and
> Bashan;
> His soul shall be satisfied on Mount
> Ephraim and Gilead."
> [Gilead at the present time is part of
> the state of Jordan.]

> "In those days and in that time," says
> the Lord,
> "The iniquity of Israel shall be sought,
> but there shall be none;
> And the sins of Judah, but they shall
> not be found;
> For I will pardon those whom I preserve."

The last word, *preserve*, might well be rendered *reserve*. God is committed to pardon the remnant He is going to reserve by His grace.

The closing words in verse 20 also agree with the promise already quoted from Isaiah 45:25: "All the descendants of Israel shall be justified."

For those who have been justified by faith in the Messiah, there remains no record of iniquity or sin.

In Ezekiel 36:22-23 God reveals one main purpose of Israel's restoration: His own glory.

> Therefore say to the house of Israel, "Thus says the Lord God: 'I do not do this for your sake, O house of Israel, but for My holy name's sake, which you have profaned among the nations wherever you went. And I will sanctify My great name, which has been profaned among the nations, which you have profaned in their midst; and the nations shall know that I am the Lord,' says the Lord God, 'when I am hallowed [or sanctified] in you before their eyes.' "

God's promise to restore Israel is not based on anything good they have done, but only that God may be glorified through it. If Israel deserved pardon and preservation, they would not need God's grace. But it is only through receiving His grace that they can restore to Him the glory which their sins have robbed from Him.

People have often said that unrepentant and unbelieving Jews will not be allowed to return to their own land. But God says that He will bring them back first and then begin to cleanse them from their sinfulness.

> For I will take you from among the nations, gather you out of all countries, and bring you into your own land. Then

> I will sprinkle clean water on you, and
> you shall be clean; I will cleanse you
> from all your filthiness and from all
> your idols. I will give you a new heart
> and put a new spirit within you; I will
> take the heart of stone out of your flesh
> and give you a heart of flesh (vv. 24-26).

I believe God has already begun the process of changing their stony hearts into hearts of flesh. It is happening right now! I have been privileged to witness firsthand some aspects of it.

In the 1940s many Jews would express their contempt for Jesus by spitting at the mention of His name. They also refused to spell His name in its correct Hebrew form.

Following the Six-Day War in 1967, however, a remarkable change in this attitude began to manifest itself. Many Jews are now ready to acknowledge that Jesus really was Jewish and seem eager to hear of the impact He has had in the lives of Gentile Christians. A Jewish professor of history, who lectures on the period of the New Testament, stated that in previous years his students had been concerned to learn only the historical facts, but now they are mainly interested in the person of Jesus Himself.

Since 1967 a whole new movement has grown up consisting of Jews who have personally acknowledged Jesus as their Messiah, while retaining their identity as Jews. The name by which they have become know is *Messianic Jews*. Worldwide, they now number in the hundreds of thousands.

God reveals that this change of heart will prepare Israel to receive the indwelling of the Holy Spirit:

> I will put My Spirit within you and cause you to walk in My statutes, and you will keep My judgments and do them. Then you shall dwell in the land that I gave to your fathers; you shall be My people, and I will be your God (vv. 27-28).

There is no doubt as to the land which God gave to the forefathers of Israel. Only one land answers to that description: the land which is now again known as Israel. I must emphasize that this promise describes a literal, historical return of the Jews to their land. There is no way to "explain away" this promise. The Bible is God's Word, and this promise must be fulfilled!

But physical restoration to the land is not the final goal. It is only a necessary prelude to the climax which is God's ultimate purpose: restoration to God Himself. "You shall be My people, and I will be your God." All the events currently taking place in the Middle East are being divinely orchestrated to bring about this supremely important objective: the reconciliation of Israel to their God.

A little further on in Ezekiel 36 God again reminds the Jewish people that they have done nothing to deserve their restoration:

> "Not for your sake do I do this," says the Lord God, "let it be known to you. Be ashamed and confounded for your own ways, O house of Israel!" (v. 32)

Ultimately, the whole human race has no hope of good apart from the mercy and grace of God. By definition, these can never be earned. This is equally true of Jews and Gentiles. God has chosen, however, to make His restoration of Israel a grand, historical demonstration of this truth to all nations.

CHAPTER FIVE

A LITTLE
PIECE OF LAND

One amazing feature of biblical revelation is the prominence it gives to a tiny strip of land at the east end of the Mediterranean, originally known as the land of Canaan. Most of the events recorded in the Bible as history, or predicted as prophecy, center around this land. In particular, it is the focus of a series of statements contained in Psalm 105:7-11. This passage opens with a declaration of God's supreme authority over the whole earth:

> He is the Lord our God;
> His judgments are in all the earth (v. 7).

The God of the Bible is Lord over the whole earth. The judgments He pronounces do not apply just to one nation or one little piece of land. His authority extends to all nations and the whole earth.

However, God has made a special, unique commitment to one human family, descended from Abraham. This commitment is summed up in verses 8-10:

> He remembers His *covenant* forever,
> The *word* which He *commanded*, for a
>   thousand generations,
> The *covenant* which He made with
>   Abraham,
> And His *oath* to Isaac,
> And confirmed it to Jacob for a *statute*,
> To Israel as an *everlasting covenant*
>   (italics added).

What an amazing Scripture passage! I know of no other that combines so many words to express a solemn commitment of God: covenant, word, commandment, oath, statute, everlasting covenant. There is no language used in the Bible that could more strongly emphasize God's total commitment.

Every covenant of God represents a solemn commitment, but this one is further described as an *everlasting* covenant. It remains in force forever. It can never be revoked.

Furthermore, it is expressed not merely by God's Word; it is confirmed by His oath. The writer of Hebrews tells us why God gives His oath: "That by two immutable [unchangeable] things, in which it is impossible for God to lie, we might have strong consolation..." (Heb. 6:18). The first unchangeable thing that God gives is His Word; the second is His oath.

The unparalleled emphasis which the psalmist

here uses to express God's commitment naturally prompts us to ask: What does it all center in? What is God so tremendously concerned about? To what is He taking pains to express His total commitment? The answer is given in this verse in Psalm 105:

> Saying, "To you I will give *the land of Canaan*
> As the allotment of your inheritance"
> (v. 11, italics added).

What is it all about? I never read this passage without being amazed that almighty God, the Creator of the universe, the King of the earth, has gone to such lengths to assert the destiny of a little piece of territory at the east end of the Mediterranean Sea. God attaches far more importance to it than most of us imagine!

Somebody else attaches a great deal of importance to it as well — and that someone is the devil. This is why the Middle East continues to draw tremendous conflict.

The verses of Psalm 105 that we have just looked at represent the title deed to the land of Canaan. Just as a title deed specifies the exact identity of the person holding the deed, God also ensures with specific language that we know to whom this land is committed. He refers to "the covenant which He made with Abraham, and His oath to Isaac, and confirmed...to Jacob, for a statute, to Israel as an everlasting covenant" (vv. 9-10). Thus, the covenant goes from Abraham through Isaac (not through Ishmael) to Jacob, whose name became Israel.

I don't know how God could have said it more clearly or emphasized it more decisively. A person has to have a "theological squint" not to see what that passage is saying. And I have to add that I believe it insults God to suggest that He doesn't know how to say what He means. To question this passage (or other similar passages) is to say, in effect, "God, I know You said it, but I don't think You really meant what You said." That is a position I would not wish to take!

I have personally studied the passages in which God gives His oath in confirmation of His word. I have concluded that it is the most emphatic form of divine declaration provided in the Bible. If Psalm 105 were the only passage of Scripture which records God's oath confirming His promise to give the land of Canaan to Israel, that would be sufficient in itself to establish this promise beyond question. But God considered this issue so important that He caused it to be recorded in the Bible in forty-six places.[*] Surely this is one of the unrecognized wonders of the Bible!

The final passage that records God's oath concerning the land of Canaan is Ezekiel 47:14: "You [Israelites] shall inherit it [the land] equally...for I raised My hand in an oath to give it to your fathers, and this land shall fall to you as your inheritance."

Beyond all question, the context indicates that the fulfillment of this promise is still in the fu-

---

[*] For a complete list of all the relevant passages, see Appendix B.

ture. This rules out any suggestion that restricts the outworking of God's oath to events that have already taken place. On the contrary, it stretches out into a future to which no limits are set. As long as the land continues to exist, its destiny will be determined by God's oath.

In the light of all these Scripture verses, it is surely surprising that anyone who accepts the authority of the Bible would raise any further questions. Nevertheless, in the article I mentioned earlier that criticized Israel and advanced the theory that we are all Jews, reference was made to a passage in Romans. Speaking about the Israelites, Paul says:

> "...to whom pertain the adoption, the glory, the covenants, the giving of the law, the service of God, and the promises..." (Rom. 9:4).

The writer of the article reasoned that because Paul speaks of the covenants and promises but makes no mention of the land, God's commitment to give the land to Israel is no longer relevant.

I find this reasoning — representative of many in the church — to be faulty. The promises in Scripture have countless references to the land, as I have already pointed out, so that if the promises are for Israel, then the land is for Israel. Furthermore, God has committed Himself by covenant with the utmost clarity to give Israel that land. The covenants, according to Paul, remain in effect.

So the conclusion that the land is no longer for Israel must be false. The land is included in both the promises and the covenants. In fact, when Paul said the promises and covenants belong to Israel, he was saying, in effect that, in many different ways the land is given *eternally* to Israel.

Another argument sometimes used by Christians is that Israel had her chance but was unfaithful and failed God. They say, therefore, that God has changed His mind and the promises given to Israel are now for the church.

When I hear this theory, I find myself mentally looking back over nineteen centuries of church history. I see an endless succession of heresy, apostasy, covetousness, immorality, continual squabbling and division and ceaseless struggles for power and preeminence. I even see professing Christians subjecting their fellow Christians to torture and cruel deaths in the name of Christ.

Add to all this sixteen or more centuries of vicious anti-Semitism, and I am left wondering: Who has been more unfaithful, Israel or the church?

If God could change His mind about His promises to Israel and take her name and give it to some other group, surely He could just as well change His mind about His promises to the church and take her title and give it to some other group. This is an important issue, then, for every Christian to consider.

In the final analysis, our confidence in God's mercy is based on His commitments in His Word and in His covenants. If God can change those commitments and annul those covenants, we are left with no security whatever as Christians. Thus, the issues of the identity and destiny of Israel concern not only the Jews but also all Gentile believers who have come to God through the new covenant in Jesus.

God's Boundaries

The God of the Bible, who is the God of the whole earth, has a plan and a place for every nation. Paul declares to the men of Athens in Acts 17:26:

> From one man he [God] made every nation of men, that they should inhabit the whole earth; and he determined the times set for them and the exact places where they should live (NIV).

If God has determined the exact places where nations should live and the times they should live there, He has a place not only for Israel but for every nation on earth. There is just one important thing to bear in mind: The place He has for Israel is not offered to any other nation.

This does not mean, however, that Arabs or other nationalities are excluded from the territory assigned to Israel. On the contrary, throughout Israel's history as a nation, God has always made specific provision for people of other nations to dwell among them, accepting both the privileges and responsibilities that doing so entails.

In Ezekiel 47:22-23 God ordains an allotment of Israel's land that is still in the future. In this passage of Scripture He makes specific provision for people of other nationalities to reside among the people of Israel and to share all their privileges:

> "It shall be that you will divide it [the land] by lot as an inheritance for yourselves, and for the strangers who dwell among you and who bear children among you. They shall be to you as native-born among the children of Israel; they shall have an inheritance with you among the tribes of Israel. And it shall be that in whatever tribe the stranger dwells, there you shall give him his inheritance," says the Lord God.

God has indeed given the land by an irrevocable covenant to Israel, but He opens the door wide for strangers from all other nations to share it with them, provided they fulfill their obligations.

In addition to this provision for strangers, however, God has given the Arabs a place of their own. At present, the Arab nations from the Atlantic to the Persian Gulf number 170 million people. They possess a land mass of 14 million square kilometers. Israel controls only 28,000 square kilometers.

In 1917 the Balfour Declaration promised to the Jewish people a certain geographical area that included the whole of what is now Jordan. Then in 1922, by a stroke of the British pen, Winston Churchill created out of that area an Arab state named Transjordan (later renamed Jordan). By that one act, 78 percent of the total area appointed for a Jewish national home was given to Arabs. Furthermore, Jews are not free to live in Jordan, while Arabs are free to live in Israel.

This means that the rest of the territory now left west of the Jordan is only 22 percent of the original inheritance offered to the Jews. Even in this area the Jews have been subjected to continual pressure and harassment, both by political agitation and by open acts of aggression.

God has warned the nations of the world, however, that a time is coming when He will call them into account for their high-handed actions in regard to the land of Israel. In Joel 3:2 He declares:

> I will also gather all nations,
> And bring them down to the Valley of
>   Jehoshaphat;
> And I will enter into judgment with
>   them there
> On account of My people, My heritage
>   Israel,
> Whom they have scattered among the
>   nations;
> They have also divided up My land.

In contemporary speech, "dividing up My land" is called *partition*. This is precisely what the United Nations did on November 29, 1947, when they voted to divide Palestine into two areas, one for Jews and one for Arabs.

A Time of Relocation

The governments of both Britain and the United States have at times sought to influence the allocation of the land of Israel. This has also been the subject of various resolutions of the United Nations. No human government, however, has the last word on this matter. Ultimately, at the appointed time, every nation on earth will occupy the place God has appointed for it.

The twentieth century has witnessed many significant developments that are related to the outworking of God's purpose to relocate the nations within the boundaries He had appointed for them. At the beginning of the century, God's time had come for the Jewish people to return to their own land. The stage was set for this by the first Zionist world conference held in 1897.

Then in 1917, one of the most significant years in world history, Jerusalem was liberated by General Edmund Allenby from four hundred years of Turkish domination, the Balfour Declaration was signed by the British government, and the first officially atheist state came into being — that is, the Soviet Union. All these events were part of God's program to close this present age.

As we look at history, however, it is clear that the Jews did not, for the most part, want to go back to Palestine. A minority was eagerly committed to it, but had it been left to the Jews themselves, few would have returned. It seemed as if God's purpose would be frustrated.

But then came the holocaust! Our minds reel at the agony and horror of it, yet in the end it served God's purposes. Nothing less would have uprooted the Jewish communities from Europe, where they had settled and lived for hundreds of years. The pressure of the holocaust impelled them to turn their faces once again to their own land.

These events illustrate two opposite sides of God's character. He is utterly faithful in His love and yet, if need be, ruthless in carrying out His predetermined purposes. In Jeremiah 31:3 God speaks to Israel and says, "Yes, I have loved you with an everlasting love...." This love turned the human wickedness of the holocaust into the occasion for Israel's rebirth as a nation. God thus fulfilled His promise in Hosea 2:15: "I will give her [Israel]...the Valley of Achor [trouble] as a door of hope."

CHAPTER SIX

IS GOD UNJUST?

Many people claim that injustice has resulted from Israel being restored to their own land. Even some sincere Christians hold this point of view. The Bible is emphatic, however, that God is incapable of injustice. In Deuteronomy 32:3-4 (NAS), in his closing words to Israel, Moses declared:

> For I proclaim the name of the Lord;
> Ascribe greatness to our God!
> The Rock! His work is perfect,
> For all His ways are just;
> A God of faithfulness and without injustice,
> Righteous and upright is He.

Someone has compared our view of history to a person looking at the reverse side of an oriental rug. The various shapes and colors seem confused and unattractive. But when the rug is turned right side up, its true beauty can be appreciated.

So it is with the outworking of God's purposes in history. From our earthly point of view it is hard to discern the pattern which God is weaving. Often it seems jumbled and meaningless. But when we are able to see it from heaven's perspective, we can agree with Moses that His work is perfect, and all His ways are just.

This is not to deny that on the human level acts of injustice have been perpetrated by the various parties involved in the return of Israel to their land. Many people have suffered greatly.

Of all the parties involved, however, none has suffered as much as the Jews. After six million of their people perished in the holocaust, a tiny remnant have had to face more than forty years of life-and-death struggle for survival in their own land.

I myself have experienced firsthand at least some small measure of both the injustice and the suffering that accompanied the rebirth of the state of Israel. During the conflict that broke out at that period, my first wife and I were living in Jerusalem with our adopted family of eight girls. Of these, six were Jewish, one was a Palestinian Arab and one was English. Their ages ranged from twenty to five. Twice within a few months, my wife and children and I had to flee from our home in the middle of the night, taking nothing more with us than what we could carry in our hands.

On the first occasion our lives were threatened by a detachment of soldiers from the Arab Legion. This was the official armed force of Jordan and one of the security forces in Jerusalem at that time, theoretically responsible to safeguard the residents of the city. At seven o'clock one evening we learned that a group of these soldiers was planning to attack our home at midnight and to rape and/or murder our Jewish girls. Our whole family walked out into the dark at nine o'clock and never returned to that house again.

At that point, my family and I became refugees. Certainly we did not suffer as much as many, yet I have had firsthand experience of both injustice and suffering. But to charge God with injustice on that account would be an error.

The problem is that under the influence of humanistic philosophy, our contemporary Western society has embraced a perverted and unbalanced view of human relationships.

The issue is brought out in Matthew 22:36-39, where a lawyer is questioning Jesus:

> "Teacher, which is the great commandment in the law?" Jesus said to him, " 'You shall love the Lord your God with all your heart, with all your soul, and with all your mind.' This is the first and great commandment. And the second is like it: 'You shall love your neighbor as yourself.' "

Here we see that God requires from us two dimensions of love — one vertical and the other horizontal. The vertical dimension is love for God; the horizontal dimension is love for our fellow human beings. But the vertical dimension is primary; the horizontal is secondary.

Furthermore, the horizontal relationship is

dependent upon the vertical. If we do not love God above all else, our love for our fellowmen can never be all that God requires.

The same is true in respect of justice. From the biblical perspective, justice has two dimensions — vertical and horizontal. The vertical dimension defines the claims that God has, as Creator, upon the whole human race. The horizontal deals with the claims that men have on their fellowmen.

The current secular approach to Middle East issues typically ignores the vertical dimension of justice. Unfortunately, many professing Christians have been influenced by this secular way of thinking. Nevertheless, true justice requires that we first acknowledge the claims that God has on all men, and only after that should we acknowledge the claims that we have on our fellowmen or that they have on us.

As we have already seen, one primary claim that God, as Creator, has on all nations is to determine the areas which He has allotted to each of them to inhabit. As long as men refuse to acknowledge this just claim of God upon them, they will never know true justice or true peace.

In Acts 17:31, speaking to a Gentile audience in Athens, Paul declared that the resurrection of Jesus from the dead marked Him out as God's appointed judge and ruler, to whom all men must give account:

> For he [God] has set a day when he will judge the world with justice by the man he has appointed. He has given proof of this to all men by raising him from the dead (NIV).

I recall a remark once by Marcus Dods, a former professor of history at Cambridge University: "The resurrection of Jesus Christ is one of the best attested facts of human history." Because God has thus attested Jesus, He requires that all men submit themselves to His authority. This is the primary, vertical dimension of justice.

When the peoples of the Middle East have acknowledged God's just claim upon their submission to Jesus, the way will be opened for them to achieve peace with each other. In the meanwhile, political negotiations can produce at best a temporary, superficial peace. True justice and lasting peace, however, will not come to the Middle East until the Messiah reigns.

Jew First, Then Gentile

The record of the holocaust, which has had such a profound effect on the destiny of Israel, also raises vitally important questions for other sectors of the human race.

If God permitted the tribulation of the holocaust to come upon the Jews, His chosen people, will He withhold tribulation of equal severity from Gentiles who have such a long record of mistreating and persecuting the Jews? Again, if God permitted the holocaust to bring the Jews of Europe into alignment with His purpose, what will He permit to come on the church if she persists in refusing to fulfill God's revealed purpose for her?

In Romans 2 Paul outlines a certain order in which God deals with humanity:

> "[God] will render to each one according to his deeds": eternal life to those who by patient continuance in doing good seek for glory, honor, and immortality; but to those who are self-seeking and do not obey the truth, but obey unrighteousness — indignation and wrath, tribulation and anguish, on every soul of man who does evil, of the Jew first and also of the Greek [or Gentile]; but glory, honor, and peace to everyone who works what is good, to the Jew first and also to the Greek [or Gentile] (vv. 6-10).

God administers both blessing and judgment in a certain order: to the Jew first and also to the Gentile. He delights to pour out blessing, and He is slow to administer judgment. Nevertheless, persistent disobedience will ultimately provoke His judgment.

Christians are ready to apply this principle to the Jews, but we need to ask ourselves: How does it apply to the church?

God's love for the church, just like His love for Israel, is everlasting. He has a plan for the church that involves tremendous blessing and privilege. At the present time, however, a great part of the professing church is not submitted to or walking in God's plan.

In Matthew 28:19-20 and Mark 16:15 Jesus commanded His followers to go into all the world and make disciples of all the nations. This command was never revoked, nor was it addressed to a small fraction of the church; it was addressed to the whole church.

There are many different ways in which Christians can play their part in carrying out this command, but the overall responsibility must be shared by the whole church. It embraces our prayers, our finances, our activities and every priority in our lives. No Christian is exempt.

When we stand before Christ's judgment seat, each one of us must be prepared to give a personal answer to the question: What part did you play in seeing that the gospel of My kingdom was proclaimed to all nations?

Yet at this present time probably less than 5 percent of the church is committed in any significant way to proclaiming the gospel of the kingdom to all nations. If challenged about this, Christians would probably come up with a variety of different answers. Here are just a few of those which might be heard:

I know God called me to Africa, but I'm married now and we want to have a family....

I wish I could give for this work, but we have so many debts — our mortgage payments are high, and we have two car payments, and we really need a VCR to watch Bible-teaching videos....

My sister is always praying, but then she has time. I'm too busy with my job and night classes....

Some of these answers sound like echoes of reasons which Jews might have given for continuing to live in Germany after Hitler came to power in 1933. The delusive appeal of comfort and security has blinded many Christians, just as many Jews were blinded to the clear indications of Hitler's diabolical schemes and even to the warnings of their own prophets.

For instance, God had said concerning them in

Jeremiah 16:15-16:

> "...I will bring them back into their land
> which I gave to their fathers. Behold, I
> will send for many fishermen," says the
> Lord, "and they shall fish them; and af-
> terward I will send for many hunters,
> and they shall hunt them from every
> mountain and every hill, and out of the
> holes of the rocks."

All this was exactly fulfilled in the years following 1933. First, God sent "fishermen" — men such
as Ze'ev Jabotinsky, one of the early Jewish pio-
neers in Palestine — who warned the Jews of
Germany: "There is no future for you here. Come
back to your own land while the doors are still
open."

Yet the Jewish leaders in Germany made light
of such warnings and continued to maintain that
they could be secure and prosperous there. By the
time they were ready to acknowledge the real
facts concerning Hitler's intentions, the doors of
escape were closed for most of them.

After that, in fulfillment of His prophetic warning, God released the "hunters" — the Nazis —
who literally "hunt[ed] them from every mountain and every hill, and out of the holes of the
rocks." Ultimately, six million Jews in Europe
perished.

It is now relatively easy for Bible-believing
Christians to see how God's warnings to the Jewish people were literally fulfilled. We need to remember, however, that there is no personal
favoritism with God. The principles of His justice

are the same for Christians as they are for Jews. God said to Israel — through the same prophet Jeremiah — "I have loved you with an everlasting love" (Jer. 31:3). Yet His love for Israel did not cause Him to withhold the judgments He had previously pronounced on them through the mouth of the same prophet.

God loves the church, too, with an everlasting love, but His love does not cancel any of the commands which He has given in the New Testament. What He desires from the church is willing, wholehearted obedience to these commands. But if He does not receive this kind of obedience, He may find another way to bring the church into line with His will.

The church at this time seems to be following the same dangerous course as the Jews of Germany when Hitler came to power. Countless Christians today are so ensnared by the delusions of comfort and security that they are ignoring the clear command of Jesus to bring the gospel of His kingdom to all nations.

Is it possible that God would permit something equivalent to a holocaust to come upon a church that stubbornly persists in ignoring His commands and His warnings?

For me this is not just a theological issue. It is a very real and urgent question, one we need to answer.

CHAPTER SEVEN

ELECTION AND THE CHURCH

We have already seen that God's dealings with Israel are the expression of His sovereign decision, not made on the basis of works. In particular, the apostle Paul emphasizes that God rejected Esau and chose Jacob while they were still in the womb to demonstrate that the basis of His dealings with nations is His own sovereign choice. Gentile Christians sometimes have difficulty accepting this principle, especially when emphasis is placed on God's choice of the Jews.

Nevertheless, a careful analysis of the New Testament reveals that exactly the same principle applies to Gentile Christians. In fact, it applies to all believers, irrespective of national or racial background. Every true believer in Jesus Christ has been divinely elected (chosen). Otherwise, he would not and could not be a believer.

Some sections of the church do not recognize

this. Those sections of the church that do recognize it are often regarded with suspicion. This may be due partly to the fact that while these believers have embraced an important truth, they have sometimes emphasized it to the point where they have ignored other equally important truths. In this way they have carried one particular truth to unbiblical extremes.

I believe there is greater imbalance in ignoring God's sovereignty and divine choice than there is in overemphasizing it. In fact, a great deal of superficiality and presumption in contemporary Christianity is due to the fact that we do not realize the divine, eternal origin of our salvation.

We are Christians not because we chose God but because God chose us. In much contemporary teaching, we are left with the feeling that salvation depends entirely on our making the right decision, when actually this is secondary. Salvation depends on the decision God has already made. Any decision we make is merely a response to the decision which God has already made. Furthermore, He made that decision before He created the world.

In other words, the principle of divine election, which we have seen applied to Israel, applies just as much to the church. God has no other principle. He never endorses or blesses any decision or program which He Himself has not initiated. Many Christians would be less insecure if they realized that their lives are products of a plan that was conceived in eternity before creation ever took place.

A number of New Testament passages, when taken together, unfold this principle of divine

election. First, in John 15:16, Jesus is speaking to
His disciples:

> You did not choose Me, but I chose you
> and appointed you that you should go
> and bear fruit, and that your fruit
> should remain, that whatever you ask
> the Father in My name He may give
> you.

The apostles had not become followers of Jesus
because they made the right choice. Jesus made
the choice, they didn't. This principle applies to
all believers whom God calls into His service. In 2
Timothy 1:9 Paul says that God "has saved us and
called us with a holy calling, not according to our
works, but according to His own purpose and
grace *which was given to us in Christ Jesus before
time began...*" (italics added).

The process of divine election is unfolded in
greater detail in Romans 8:29-30:

> For whom He [God] foreknew, He also
> predestined to be conformed to the im-
> age of His Son.... Moreover whom He
> predestined, these He also called; whom
> He called, these He also justified; and
> whom He justified, these He also glori-
> fied.

This passage contains a succession of verbs in
the past tense: foreknew, predestined, called, justified, glorified. They mark the only route that
leads to God's glory. The first two stages — foreknew and predestined — occurred in eternity be-

fore time began.

The whole process had its origin in God's fore-knowledge. From eternity He foreknew each one of us. On the basis of this He predestined us — that is, He planned the course that our lives should take.

Personally, I am very grateful for this. Only in eternity will I know what calamities would have befallen me had I directed my own life. Even more important, eternity will reveal the fruit which came forth because I sought to follow God's plan and obey His direction.

The first epistle of Peter sheds further light on this process. It is important, however, to recognize that this epistle is addressed "to the pilgrims of the Dispersion" (1 Pet. 1:1). The word *dispersion* (in Greek, *diaspora*) was regularly used to refer specifically to Jews living outside the land of Israel. Thus, this epistle (along with Hebrews, James and 2 Peter) is addressed primarily to Jewish believers. Nevertheless, the truth it presents applies equally to all believers.

> To the pilgrims [or strangers] of the Dispersion in Pontus, Galatia, Cappadocia, Asia, and Bithynia, elect according to the foreknowledge of God the Father....

The word *elect* is the same as *chosen* in modern English. Thus Peter discloses one more stage of the process that occurred in eternity: God chose us. If we combine these words of Peter with the words of Paul in Romans 8:29-30, we find that there are actually three stages that belong to eternity, before time began: God foreknew us; He chose us; He predestined us.

This revelation of God's foreknowledge is needed to complete the revelation of His choice. Without this, we could conclude that God's choice is purely arbitrary. But this is not so. His choice of every individual proceeds out of His foreknowledge. He knows exactly what He can make of each life.

Many times a person who is called by God to some special task feels entirely inadequate — as did Moses, Gideon, Jeremiah and many others. The temptation is to respond, "But, God, I can't do that!"

However, God has already given His answer in Scripture: I knew you before creation took place. My choice and My calling are based on My knowledge of you. I know what I can make of you better than you yourself, and I have arranged the course of your life accordingly (see Ps. 139:13-16).

People may react in different ways to this revelation from God's Word. My own response is the very opposite of pride or presumption. I have an awesome sense of personal responsibility. My greatest concern is to fulfill the plan God worked out for me in eternity. I begin to identify with the words of Jesus in John 4:34: "My food is to do the will of Him who sent Me, and to finish His work."

On the other hand, my sense of responsibility is balanced by the wonderful assurance of 1 Thessalonians 5:24: "He who calls you is faithful, who also will do it." The outcome is an acknowledgement of moment-by-moment dependence on God's all-sufficient grace.

Some who read this may want to apply it to their own lives yet be held back by a sense of their own inadequacy. To each one of these I would offer a word of encouragement, based on more than fifty years in the Lord's service: Look away from yourself and your own ability, and trust yourself to God's omnipotence.

The psalmist David also has a word of counsel for you:

> Commit your way to the Lord,
> Trust also in Him,
> And He shall bring it to pass (Ps. 37:5).

I can testify from experience: It works!

Not Effort, But Union

In Ephesians 1 Paul further emphasizes that, as Christians, we have been chosen by God from eternity.

> Blessed be the God and Father of our Lord Jesus Christ, who has blessed us with every spiritual blessing in the heavenly places in Christ, just as He chose us in Him before the foundation of the world, that we should be holy and without blame before Him in love, having predestined us to adoption as sons by Jesus Christ to Himself, according to the good pleasure of His will... (vv. 3-5).

Paul continues in verse 11:

> In Him also we have obtained an inheritance, being predestined according to

the purpose of Him who works all things according to the counsel of His will....

Note the sequence of verbs in the past tense in these verses: He chose us; He predestined us; we have been predestined.... All this is "according to the purpose of Him who works all things according to the counsel of His will." There is no mention of human choice or human merit. All the way through, from eternity and on into time, the initiative proceeds from God.

The ultimate purpose to be achieved is that "we should be holy and without blame before Him in love." How could any of us ever aspire to achieve this by our own efforts?

One of the great enemies of true holiness is religious activity. The key to Christian success is not effort; it is union. Jesus said, "I am the vine, you are the branches" (John 15:5). Branches do not put forth any effort to produce grapes. A branch is able to produce grapes because the sap rises up through the trunk into the branches as the sun shines upon it. In that simple parable we have a beautiful picture of the three persons of the Godhead: the Father is the vinedresser; Jesus is the vine; and the Holy Spirit is the life-giving nourishment.

The key to fruitfulness is to abide in Jesus, content in the knowledge that God will bring about in your life that which He has ordained. This is true New Testament holiness.

This brief analysis of the doctrine of election (God's choice) in the New Testament brings out one important point, which has often been overlooked: The basis of God's dealings with the church is exactly the same as the basis of His dealings with Israel. In each case, it is God who foreknows, God who chooses, God who predestines.

Christians who object to the teaching that Israel has been irreversibly chosen by God actually undermine the basis of their own relationship with God. In the final analysis, Israel and the church are both equally dependent on the free, unmerited favor of God, expressed in His choice and His calling. The words of Paul in Romans 11:29 apply equally to Jews and to Christians: "the gifts and the calling of God are irrevocable."

CHAPTER EIGHT

WILL THE CHURCH ALSO BE A REMNANT?

In Romans 11:26 Paul says, "All Israel will be saved." But earlier in Romans 9:27 he had said, "The remnant will be saved." In other words, the "all Israel" who will be saved will be the remnant whom God has foreknown.

Passages explained previously in this book, such as Zephaniah 3:12-13 and Zechariah 13:8-9, confirm that the chosen ones of Israel will be a remnant — perhaps one-third. We have seen, too, that the basis of God's dealings with the church is the same as with Israel. We therefore need to ask ourselves one vitally important question: *Will the church that is saved also be a remnant?*

God promises a truly glorious future to Israel, but He also warns that the saved remnant of Israel will have gone through intense pressure to make them what He intends them to be. Will the church likewise emerge as a remnant that has been purified by a pressure that is no less intense?

Several Scripture passages concerning the church seem to depict a remnant that has fulfilled certain conditions. In Luke 13:24-27 Jesus addresses the question: Are there few who are saved? He says:

> Strive to enter through the narrow gate, for many, I say to you, will seek to enter and will not be able. When once the Master of the house has risen up and shut the door, and you begin to stand outside and knock at the door, saying, "Lord, Lord, open for us," and He will answer and say to you, "I do not know you, where you are from," then you will begin to say, "We ate and drank in Your presence, and You taught in our streets." But He will say, "I tell you I do not know you, where you are from. Depart from Me, all you workers of iniquity [lawlessness]."

At the close of the Sermon on the Mount, Jesus gives a similar warning:

> Not everyone who says to Me, "Lord, Lord," shall enter the kingdom of heaven, but he who does the will of My Father in heaven. Many will say to Me in that day, "Lord, Lord, have we not prophesied in Your name, cast out demons in Your name, and done many wonders in Your name?" And then I will

declare to them, "I never knew you; depart from Me, you who practice lawlessness!" (Matt. 7:21-23).

Personally, I do not believe that these self-proclaimed miracle workers in Jesus' example were lying. They had actually done what they claimed. But being able to prophesy, cast out demons and work wonders does not necessarily prove that a person is one of God's elect.

In the Lord's answer to these people one significant comment occurs three times: "I do not know you...I do not know you...I never knew you." They had never been on the list of God's elect. From His perspective in eternity He had looked below their public ministry into their personal lives. He had searched for the nature of Jesus, the Lamb, manifested in meekness and purity and holiness. But He searched in vain!

Outwardly, these miracle workers had been busy serving the Lord, but in their innermost character God had discerned something described as "lawlessness." This expressed itself in attitudes such as pride, arrogance, self-seeking, covetousness, personal ambition. For such, He had no place reserved in heaven. God has one unvarying requirement that runs through the whole Bible: without holiness no one will see the Lord (see Heb. 12:14).

In Matthew 24 Jesus reveals another mark which characterizes God's elect: endurance. In verses 4-13 He gives a brief but vivid picture of the period leading up to the close of the present age. He describes a series of events which He calls "birth pangs" or "labor pains" because they climax in the birth of God's kingdom on earth. He warns His disciples that they will be subjected to progressively increasing pressures.

> Then they will deliver you up to tribulation and kill you, and you will be hated by all nations for My name's sake (v. 9).

What sort of people are described here? Clearly they are Christians who suffer "for [His] name's sake."

> And then many will be offended, will betray one another, and will hate one another. Then many false prophets will rise up and deceive many. And because lawlessness will abound, the love of many will grow cold (vv. 10-12).

Who are the "many" who will be offended and betray one another? Many Christians. And who are the many whose love — in Greek, *agape* — will grow cold because of abounding lawlessness? Again, many Christians.

In verse 13 Jesus follows with words which are both a warning and a promise: "But he who endures to the end shall be saved." Actually, the Greek is more precise: "He who *has endured* to the end will be saved." Enduring to the end is a requirement for salvation.

It is important to acknowledge that Christians in many parts of the world are already being subjected to tests of this kind. All the things that Jesus speaks of in Matthew 24:9-13 have actually been happening to Christians in communist lands, such as China (where one-fifth of the world's population is located), and in many Muslim nations. In this century, Christians in the Western nations for the most part have been exempted from tests of this kind, but there is no guarantee that this will continue.

A divine purpose is behind these tests, to which both Jews and Christians are being subjected. As the present age draws to a close, God intends to bring forth a people for His name, who will be fit to share His kingdom throughout eternity. Therefore He will not spare His people any test that is needed to produce the kind of commitment and character that He requires. The same period of testing that faces Israel likewise faces the church.

This is not a time, therefore, for Christians to stand back and say, "Let the Jews go through it; they deserve it." Rather all of us — whether Jews or Christians — need to ask ourselves: Are we prepared to go through what it will take to make us what God intends us to be? For those who make the right response, the end result will be a people who are pleasing to God, fit to share His glory.

The Response God Requires

What, then, is the response God requires?

First of all, we need to heed the warning of 2 Peter 1:19-21:

> And we have the word of the prophets made more certain, and you will do well to pay attention to it, as to a light shin-

ing in a dark place, until the day dawns and the morning star rises in your hearts. Above all, you must understand that no prophecy of Scripture came about by the prophet's own interpretation. For prophecy never had its origin in the will of man, but men spoke from God as they were carried along by the Holy Spirit (NIV).

Certainly the world around us answers to Peter's description: "a dark place." In spite of all man's technological achievements, the spiritual darkness is deepening. The hearts of men and women are filled with perplexity and uncertainty, fearful of what lies ahead. Nowhere is this truer than in the Middle East.

Nevertheless, in the midst of the darkness, God has provided one clear light: "the word of the prophets." As the surrounding darkness increases, the light of biblical prophecy grows correspondingly brighter. It is the only reliable source of information concerning Israel and the Middle East.

Living as we do in Jerusalem, Ruth and I realize that we are continually subjected to many negative forces, both religious and political. We have come to understand that we could never survive spiritually if we were to take our focus off the Scriptures. These — and these alone — provide light in the surrounding darkness.

Two Scripture verses have become particularly vivid to us, one from the Old Testament and one from the New.

> In the fear of the Lord there is strong
> confidence,
> And His children will have a place of
> refuge (Prov. 14:26).
>
> Therefore do not cast away your confi-
> dence, which has great reward (Heb.
> 10:35).

In the midst of tensions and hostilities that are never relaxed, "the word of the prophets" still provides a source of deep, untroubled confidence. We see more and more clearly, as events unfold, that God is continually at work, according to His promise given to Jeremiah: "I am watching to see that my word is fulfilled" (Jer. 1:12, NIV).

Scripture warns us against one particular attitude, and that is pride. I alluded earlier to the passage in Romans in which Paul talks about the olive tree that has as its roots Abraham, Isaac and Jacob, and which grew up as God's people Israel. Speaking to believers from a Gentile background, he explains how Gentiles came to have a place in the olive tree:

> Some of the branches were broken off,
> and you, being a wild olive tree, were
> grafted in among them, and with them
> became a partaker of the root and fat-
> ness of the olive tree... (Rom. 11:17).

Normally in horticulture a good branch is grafted into a wild tree so that the strength of the wild tree helps the good branch bring forth fruit. The reverse of this, grafting a wild branch into a good tree, is contrary to nature. For my part, I am deeply grateful to God that He took pains to graft me, as a Gentile, into His olive tree. As a Gentile, I realize that in many ways my attitudes and traditions are out of harmony with the tree itself. I am amazed at God's grace that He was, and still is, so patient with me.

It is crucial that we who are from a Gentile background maintain such an attitude of humility. Listen to Paul's message to the wild olive branches:

> ...do not boast against the branches. But if you do boast, remember that you do not support the root, but the root supports you. You will say then, "Branches were broken off that I might be grafted in." Well said. Because of unbelief they were broken off, and you stand by faith. Do not be haughty, but fear. For if God did not spare the natural branches, He may not spare you either. Therefore consider the goodness and severity of God: on those who fell, severity; but toward you, goodness, if you continue in His goodness. Otherwise you also will be cut off (Rom. 11:18-22).

Paul's message leaves no room for pride or presumption or carelessness in either Jew or Gentile. It represents a strong warning to all, but especially to those from a Gentile background.

What, then, should be our attitude toward current developments in the Middle East?

First of all, we need to take note of how accurate and up-to-date are the prophecies of Israel's regathering. In Isaiah 43:5-6 the Lord makes the following promises to Israel:

> Fear not, for I am with you;
> I will bring your descendants from the
>   east,
> And gather you from the west;
> I will say to the north, "Give them up!"
> And to the south, "Do not keep them
>   back!"
> Bring My sons from afar,
> And My daughters from the ends of the
>   earth....

The last two geographical areas designated are the north and the south. To understand the points of the compass as the Scripture refers to them, we always need to place ourselves mentally in the place which is central to all biblical revelation — that is, the land of Israel. Thus, the north is north of Israel — primarily the western half of the former Soviet Union; the south is south of Israel — primarily the eastern half of Africa.

In the years since 1989 there has been a dramatic fulfillment of these particular prophecies. By the end of 1991 almost 400,000 Jews had returned to Israel from the former Soviet Union and 20,000 from Ethiopia. In both these nations, under the influence of communism, strong political forces had opposed the release of the Jews. Yet suddenly the opposition was set aside, and the way was open for the Jews to leave.

The decisive factor that brought this about was not political but spiritual. It was God's prophetic declaration: "I will say to the north, 'Give them up!' and to the south, 'Do not keep them back.' " When the time came for the fulfillment of this prophetic word, even the strongest and most stubborn of governments had to bow before it. The north had no alternative but to "give them up." The south was no longer able to "keep them back."

For several years before all this took place, Christians around the world had seen the relevance of these prophecies in Isaiah 43:5-6. Consequently, they set themselves to pray earnestly for God to fulfill the promises He had given. The historical outcome is a demonstration that the power of believing prayer, based on Scripture, is ultimately irresistible.

Further on in the prophetic Scriptures, Jeremiah fills in many details of this end-time restoration of Israel. By way of introduction, he says:

> "For behold, the days are coming," says the Lord, "that I will bring back from captivity My people Israel and Judah," says the Lord. "And I will cause them to return to the land that I gave to their fathers, and they shall possess it" (Jer. 30:3).

As with Psalm 105, this passage leaves no doubt as to the territory referred to. God declares that He will bring Israel back to "the land that I gave to their fathers." As stated previously, only one land answers to that description — the one which is once again called by the name of Israel.

Further on, Jeremiah describes a threefold response which the Lord requires from those who have received this prophetic word of Israel's restoration:

> For thus says the Lord:
> "Sing with gladness for Jacob,
> And shout among the chief of the nations;
> Proclaim, give praise, and say,
> 'O Lord, save Your people,
> The remnant of Israel!' " (Jer. 31:7)

Here, then, are three ways in which God requires us to respond: to proclaim, to praise and to pray.

CHAPTER NINE

OUR RESPONSIBILITY

Proclaim!

One of the most effective spiritual weapons that God has put at the disposal of His people is the proclamation of His Word. The proclaimed Word of God is for us today what the rod of Moses was in his generation. With his outstretched rod Moses defeated the magicians of Egypt, stripped Pharaoh of his power, humiliated Egypt's gods and brought Israel out from slavery into freedom.

We must learn to use God's Word as Moses used his rod. As we take hold of the Scriptures and proclaim them with bold faith, we can extend God's authority into any situation where Satan opposes the people and the purposes of God.

This applies particularly to the current situation in the Middle East. Many forces oppose the revealed purposes of God, especially those connected with Israel's restoration. God does not intend, however, that His believing people should stand by as passive spectators on the sidelines of history. He expects us to take up the rod of His Word and stretch it out by bold proclamation against every force and every situation that resists His purposes.

In Jeremiah 31:10 God has given us a specific word to proclaim to all nations:

> Hear the word of the Lord, O nations [Gentiles],
> And declare it in the isles afar off, and say,
> "He who scattered Israel will gather him,
> And keep him as a shepherd does [keeps] his flock."

This word is to be proclaimed to the Gentile nations, even in the remotest parts of the earth. All the peoples of the earth are to be confronted with God's purpose concerning Israel.

The message itself is simple. It may be formulated in three successive statements. First, God scattered Israel (from their own land). Second, the same God who scattered Israel is now regathering them (to their own land). Third, God will not merely regather them; He will also keep (protect) them. Thus the ultimate safety of Israel is guaranteed by God.

I love the words of Jeremiah 31:10 in the original language because Hebrew has a unique way of condensing things. The statement "He who scattered Israel will gather him" is expressed in only three words: *Mzareh Yisrael yekabbetzenu.*

Mzareh: the one who scatters

Yisrael: Israel

Yekabbetzenu: will gather him.

Interestingly enough, that verb *yekabbetz* is directly connected with the word *kibbutz.* It is almost as if God said, "When I bring them back, I will gather them in *kibbutzim.*"

Israel is in a desperate situation, but we do not need to fear their outcome as a nation, because the same God who is gathering Israel — which is exciting enough! — will also keep them. Let us proclaim it — boldly and continually!

This passage in Jeremiah 31:10, however, is only one of many that may be used in proclamation concerning the Middle East. I will just mention briefly three others which Ruth and I proclaim regularly.

> Let all those who hate Zion
> Be put to shame and turned back.
> Let them be as the grass on the house-
> tops,
> Which withers before it grows up... (Ps.
> 129:5-6).

"Those who hate Zion" is a brief but comprehensive description of the various forces currently arrayed against Israel.

> The scepter of the wicked will not re-
> main over the land allotted to the
> righteous... (Ps. 125:3, NIV).

"The scepter of the wicked" is, I believe, an accurate description of Islam.

Finally, there is a passage in Psalm 33 which is longer but singularly appropriate to the current situation in the world and especially in the Middle East:

> Let all the earth fear the Lord;
> Let all the inhabitants of the world
> stand in awe of Him.
> For He spoke, and it was done;
> He commanded, and it stood fast.
> The Lord brings the counsel of the nations to nothing;
> He makes the plans of the peoples of no effect.
> The counsel of the Lord stands forever,
> The plans of His heart to all generations.
> Blessed is the nation whose God is the Lord,
> The people He has chosen as His own inheritance (Ps. 33:8-12).

Here is an unequivocal declaration that God's word brought the world into being, and that same word directs the course of history. Nations and their governments may hold their councils and issue their decrees, but whenever these are in opposition to God's prophetic Word, they will come to nothing. God will fulfill all His counsel and His promises concerning Israel, the people whom He has chosen as His own inheritance.

Praise!

A second spiritual weapon of measureless power is praise. In Psalm 8:2 David says to the Lord:

> Out of the mouth of babes and nursing
>   infants
> You have ordained strength...
> That You may silence the enemy and
>   the avenger.

What is it that proceeds from the mouth and is the "ordained strength" of God's people? A precise answer to this question is provided by Jesus Himself in Matthew 21:15-16. The chief priests and scribes were disturbed by the children crying out in the temple, "Hosanna to the Son of David!" and they wanted Jesus to silence them. In reply, however, Jesus referred to the words of Psalm 8:2: "Have you never read, 'Out of the mouth of babes and nursing infants You have perfected praise'?"

In this quotation Jesus made one significant change. In place of the words *ordained strength* He said *perfected praise*. This divine commentary reveals that the ordained strength of God's people is perfected praise. When this strength is released through the mouths of even those who are by nature the weakest — babes and infants — its effect is to silence "the enemy and the avenger." This last phrase is, of course, a description of the great enemy of God and man: Satan.

How important it is for us to lay hold of this truth! We do not have to passively endure the arrogant claims and lying slanders of those whom

Satan uses as channels of his venom. God has given us a weapon that can strip them of their power to do harm. It is the weapon referred to in Jeremiah 31:7 — the weapon of singing and shouting — the weapon of loud, sustained and jubilant praise offered from believing hearts through sanctified lips. When we, as God's people, make this response, He will intervene on our behalf in ways that will astonish us.

In 2 Chronicles 20 we are confronted by a dramatic demonstration of the power of praise. Jehoshaphat, king of Judah, learned that his kingdom was being invaded from the east by a vast army. He knew that he had neither the men nor the resources to engage such a force. He therefore chose to make a spiritual response; he called his people together for united fasting and prayer.

As the people were praying, a Levite gave forth a prophetic utterance:

> Do not be afraid or discouraged because of this vast army. For the battle is not yours, but God's.... You will not have to fight this battle. Take up your positions; stand firm and see the deliverance the Lord will give you, O Judah and Jerusalem. Do not be afraid; do not be discouraged. Go out to face them tomorrow, and the Lord will be with you (2 Chron. 20:15,17, NIV).

Jehoshaphat and his people received this message with heads bowed in worship. The next day,

> Jehoshaphat appointed men to sing to the Lord and to praise him for the splendor of his holiness as they went out at the head of the army, saying: "Give thanks to the Lord, for his love endures forever" (2 Chron. 20:21, NIV).

At this point there had been no change in the military situation. God's people were still hopelessly outnumbered. To offer praise in such circumstances was purely a response of faith, based on the prophetic word which they had received from God. But the record continues:

> As they began to sing and praise, the Lord set ambushes against the men of Ammon and Moab and Mount Seir who were invading Judah, and they were defeated. The men of Ammon and Moab rose up against the men from Mount Seir to destroy and annihilate them. After they finished slaughtering the men from Seir, they helped to destroy one another.
> When the men of Judah came to the place that overlooks the desert and looked toward the vast army, they saw only dead bodies lying on the ground; no one had escaped. So Jehoshaphat and his men went to carry off their plunder... (2 Chron. 20:22-25, NIV).

The same kind of response to God's prophetic word can still call forth His supernatural intervention on behalf of Israel today.

Pray!

Following after proclamation and praise, God requires a third response as He gathers Israel: prayer. Jeremiah 31:7 contains an excellent example of how we can pray:

> O Lord, save Your people,
> The remnant of Israel!

Clearly this means to pray for the salvation of Israel. God is precise in what He requires. He does not merely say, "Pray for Israel," but specifically, "Pray for their salvation."

In Ezekiel 36:37 we find another example of a prayer in which God Himself reveals what He requires His people to pray for:

> Thus says the Lord God: "I will also let the house of Israel inquire of Me to do this for them: I will increase their men like a flock."

The King James Version puts it more strongly:

> I will yet for this be inquired of by the house of Israel, to do it for them; I will increase them with men like a flock.

Reading Ezekiel 36 from verse 23 through 37 in Hebrew, I once counted that God says eighteen times in succession, "I will...." Never once does He suggest that His actions in restoring Israel proceed from any other source than His own will.

But verse 37 — the closing verse of that section

— brings out the delicate balance between God's predetermined purpose and man's response. God is saying, in effect, "Even though what I am going to do is settled, I will not do it until the house of Israel asks Me to do it for them."

This underlines the supreme purpose of prayer. It is not that we should get God to do what we want. It is that we may become instruments through which God can do what He wants. Here in Ezekiel 36:37 is a perfect example. Israel is not asked to improvise a prayer or to make her own choice. God has already declared what He will do. He waits, however, for Israel to come into agreement with His will and ask Him to do what He has already committed Himself to do.

Meanwhile, God is giving Christians from Gentile backgrounds the responsibility and the privilege to "stand in the gap" on behalf of Israel. This they do by pleading on Israel's behalf for the mercies promised them by God but which the majority of Israelites are not yet in a position to apprehend by their own faith.

A good friend of ours told the following story when he returned from a trip to Singapore. He met a fellow Christian there who had been visiting the Christians in China and had been present at one of their prayer meetings. He was particularly impressed by the intense emotion with which one of the local Christians was praying. Tears poured from his eyes and drenched his T-shirt.

So the visitor turned to his interpreter and asked, "What is he praying for?"

"He's praying for Israel," came the reply.

Such prayer had to be supernatural in origin because the Chinese at that time had received very little Bible teaching and had no way of getting real information about Israel. Such information as came to them from communist sources probably had a negative bias.

Yet this occurrence in China is not an isolated example. Christian groups in various other nations have received a similar supernatural burden to intercede for Israel. For instance, on a recent visit to Kenya I found African Christians who were deeply concerned about and praying for Israel. So far as I could determine, they had not received any specific preaching on this subject. Their motivation proceeded directly from the Holy Spirit.

It seems that in this critical hour the Holy Spirit is placing renewed emphasis upon the debt which all Gentile Christians owe to the Jewish people. (I speak as a Gentile Christian myself.)

In John 4:22 Jesus stated a simple but profound truth: "Salvation is of the Jews." This statement expresses objective historical facts. Without the Jews there would have been no patriarchs, no prophets, no apostles, no Bible and — above all — no Savior. Salvation — and every spiritual blessing that accompanies it — has come to the Gentiles through one and the same channel: the Jewish people.

As Gentiles, we have no way to repay this debt. However, we have various ways in which we can at least acknowledge it. One of the most important is by fervent, heartfelt intercession for Israel, firmly based on the prophetic Scriptures. In this way we can enter into the wonderful experience of being workers together with God for the final restoration of Israel.

CHAPTER TEN

THE CLIMAX

U p to this point we have been considering Israel and the church as if they have always been two separate entities, but this is not really the way it is. When the church first came into being, its membership was exclusively Israelite. In fact, when people who were not Jewish began to seek membership in the church, it created a crisis. The Jewish believers had to decide whether Gentiles could be admitted to the church, and if so, upon what conditions. Their conclusion is recorded in Acts 15:22-29: Gentiles who fulfilled certain simple conditions could be members — together with the Jewish believers — of one body, the church.

Early in the second century, however, the great majority of the Jewish people, having rejected the claim of Jesus to be the Messiah, completely separated themselves from the church. As a result, the church became progressively more and more Gentile in character. Nevertheless, throughout all the succeeding centuries significant numbers of Jews have always acknowledged Jesus as their Messiah and have taken their place as members of the church.

In the latter part of the twentieth century there has been a dramatic increase in the number of Jews who have acknowledged Jesus as their Messiah. Many of these have, however, been careful to maintain their historical identity as Jews. As a result, a distinct group of believers, characterized as "Messianic Jews," have grown up within the overall body of the church.

In Romans 11:25-26 Paul is speaking primarily to Gentile Christians, and he shares with them a "mystery" — that is, a purpose of God which had been kept secret but is now revealed to believers:

> For I do not desire, brethren, that you should be ignorant of this mystery, lest you should be wise in your own opinion, that blindness in part has happened to Israel until the fullness [full number] of the Gentiles has come in. And so all Israel will be saved, as it is written:
>
> The Deliverer will come out of Zion, And He will turn away ungodliness from Jacob; For this is My covenant with them, When I take away their sins.

This passage reveals two successive stages in God's plan to bring the present age to a close.

First, the words of Jesus in Matthew 24:14

must be fulfilled: "And this gospel of the kingdom will be preached in all the world as a witness to all the nations, and then the end will come."

Second, when the complete number of the Gentiles has been brought into the church, then God will once again turn fully to the preserved remnant of Israel and will reveal Himself to them in mercy and saving grace.

It appears that the transition from the emphasis on the Gentiles to the emphasis on the Jews will not be a single instantaneous event but will be gradual and progressive. We are already in the early stages of this transition.

The critical point of the Lord's revelation to Israel is prophetically depicted in Zechariah 12:10:

> And I will pour on the house of David and on the inhabitants of Jerusalem the Spirit of grace and supplication; then they will look on Me whom they pierced. Yes, they will mourn for Him as one mourns for his only son, and grieve for Him as one grieves for a firstborn.

At this point, for the first time, Israel as a nation will receive a supernatural revelation of the identity of the Messiah who had been pierced with the nails of crucifixion.

Two chapters further on, Zechariah pictures the actual return of the Messiah in person:

> And in that day His feet will stand on
>   the Mount of Olives,
> Which faces Jerusalem on the east.

And the Mount of Olives shall be split
  in two,
From east to west,
Making a very large valley;
Half of the mountain shall move to-
  ward the north
And half of it toward the south....
Thus the Lord my God will come,
And all the saints with You (Zech.
  14:4-5).

In the final pages of my book *The Last Word on the Middle East* (Derek Prince Ministries, 1982), I endeavored to lift the veil momentarily on this closing scene in the drama of Israel and the church:

In this closing scene, all the actors in the drama of establishing God's Kingdom on earth are brought together on stage. It is the same stage on which every previous crisis of the same drama has been enacted: Jerusalem and the mountains that surround it. Angelic hosts, glorified saints and the preserved remnant of Israel take their respective places.

But the central figure, outshining all the rest and drawing them together around Himself, is that of Messiah, the King.

Thus heaven will vindicate the confession that every orthodox Jew has maintained through the long centuries — even on his way to the stake or to the gas chamber:

I believe with perfect faith in the coming of the Messiah; and even if he tarries, still I will wait every day for him to come.

Thus, too, will heaven answer the prayer of the aged apostle John on the Isle of Patmos — the prayer echoed by every true Christian as he closes his New Testament:

Amen. Come, Lord Jesus.

Conclusions

The foregoing analysis of the destiny of Israel and the church, as unfolded in the Scriptures, leads us to certain important conclusions.

First, the only reliable source of light upon the current situation in the Middle East is provided by God's prophetic word. If we do not seek the light that comes from this source, we will inevitably find ourselves in the dark, subject to many forms of confusion and deception.

Second, the destiny of both Israel and the church has been determined by God in eternity on the basis of His foreknowledge. Its outworking in time is guaranteed by the irrevocable covenants which God has established with each of them.

Third, for all the good that God has promised to Israel and the church, both are equally and totally dependent upon God's grace, which can be appropriated only by faith.

Fourth, tremendous tests and pressures lie

ahead for both Israel and the church, but those who faithfully endure will be privileged to share God's kingdom with Him throughout eternity.

Fifth, Christians from Gentile backgrounds owe their entire spiritual inheritance to Israel. One appropriate way for them to acknowledge their indebtedness is to stand by Israel in the midst of their present pressures and to uphold them with faithful intercession.

Sixth, the peoples of the Middle East will never know true justice or lasting peace until they are submitted to God's appointed ruler, the Lord Jesus Christ.

APPENDIX A

This appendix lists the seventy-nine occurrences of the words *Israel* and *Israelite(s)* in the New Testament. References for verses that have been derived from Old Testament sources are indicated. (Italics have been added.)

1. Matthew 2:6
    "a Ruler Who will shepherd My people *Israel*" (cited from Mic. 5:2)

2. Matthew 2:20
    "the land of *Israel*"

3. Matthew 2:21
    "the land of *Israel*"

4. Matthew 8:10
   "not found such great faith, not even in *Israel*"

5. Matthew 9:33
   "never seen like this in *Israel*"

6. Matthew 10:6
   "to the lost sheep of the house of *Israel*"

7. Matthew 10:23
   "not have gone through the cities of *Israel* before the Son of Man comes"

8. Matthew 15:24
   "except to the lost sheep of the house of *Israel*"

9. Matthew 15:31
   "they glorified the God of *Israel*"

10. Matthew 19:28
    "will also sit on twelve thrones, judging the twelve tribes of *Israel*"

11. Matthew 27:9
    "whom they of the children of *Israel* priced" (cited from Zech. 11:12-13)

12. Matthew 27:42
    "If He is the King of *Israel*, let Him now come down"

13. Mark 12:29
    "Hear, O *Israel*" (cited from Deut. 6:4-5)

14. Mark 15:32
    "Let the Christ, the King of *Israel*, descend now from the cross"

15. Luke 1:16
    "And he will turn many of the children of *Israel*"

16. Luke 1:54
    "He has helped His servant *Israel*" (derived from Is. 41:8)

17. Luke 1:68
    "Blessed is the Lord God of *Israel*"

18. Luke 1:80
    "till the day of his manifestation to *Israel*"

19. Luke 2:25
    "waiting for the Consolation of *Israel*"

20. Luke 2:32
    "A light to bring revelation to the Gentiles, and the glory of Your people *Israel*" (cited from Is. 49:6)

21. Luke 2:34
    "the fall and rising of many in *Israel*"

22. Luke 4:25
    "many widows were in *Israel*"

23. Luke 4:27
    "many lepers were in *Israel*"

24. Luke 7:9
    "not found such great faith, not even in *Israel*"

25. Luke 22:30
    "sit on thrones judging the twelve tribes of *Israel*"

26. Luke 24:21
    "He who was going to redeem *Israel*"

27. John 1:31
    "that He should be revealed to *Israel*"

28. John 1:47
    "an *Israelite* indeed" (Jesus referring to Nathanael)

29. John 1:49
    "You are the King of *Israel*"

30. John 3:10
    "Are you the teacher of *Israel*"

31. John 12:13
    "Blessed is...the King of *Israel*"

32. Acts 1:6
    "restore the kingdom to *Israel*"

33. Acts 2:22
    "Men of *Israel*" (literally, *Israelites*)

34. Acts 2:36
    "Therefore let all the house of *Israel* know"

35. Acts 3:12
    "Men of *Israel*" (literally, *Israelites*)

36. Acts 4:8
    "Rulers of the people and elders of *Israel*"

37. Acts 4:10
    "let it be known to...all the people of *Israel*"

38. Acts 4:27
    "with the Gentiles and the people of *Israel*"

39. Acts 5:21
    "all the elders of the children of *Israel*"

40. Acts 5:31
    "to give repentance to *Israel*"

41. Acts 5:35
    "Men of *Israel*" (literally, *Israelites*)

42. Acts 7:23
    "to visit his brethren, the children of *Israel*"

43. Acts 7:37
    "Moses who said to the children of *Israel*"

44. Acts 7:42
    "Did you offer Me...O house of *Israel*" (cited from Amos 5:25-27)

45. Acts 9:15
    "to bear My name before Gentiles, kings, and the children of *Israel*"

46. Acts 10:36
    "The word which God sent to the children of *Israel*"

47. Acts 13:16
    "Men of *Israel*" (literally, *Israelites*)

48. Acts 13:17
    "The God of this people *Israel*"

49. Acts 13:23
    "God raised up for *Israel* a Savior"

50. Acts 13:24
    "the baptism of repentance to all the people of *Israel*"

51. Acts 21:28
    "Men of *Israel*" (literally, *Israelites*)

52. Acts 28:20
    "for the hope of *Israel* I am bound"

53. Romans 9:3-4
    "my countrymen...who are *Israelites*"

54/55. Romans 9:6
"They are not all *Israel* who are of *Israel*"*

56. Romans 9:27
"Isaiah also cries out concerning *Israel*"

57. Romans 9:27
"Though the number of the children of *Israel* be as the sand" (cited from Is. 10:22-23)

58. Romans 9:31
"but *Israel*, pursuing the law of righteousness"

59. Romans 10:1
"my...prayer to God for *Israel*"

60. Romans 10:19
"did *Israel* not know?"

61. Romans 10:21
"But to *Israel* he says"

62. Romans 11:1
"For I also am an *Israelite*"

63. Romans 11:2
"he pleads with God against *Israel*"

---

* This usage restricts the meaning of *Israel* or *Israelite* to only those Israelites who have fulfilled certain spiritual requirements (see chapter 1).

64. Romans 11:7
    "*Israel* has not obtained what it seeks"

65. Romans 11:25
    "blindness in part has happened to *Israel*"

66. Romans 11:26
    "And so all *Israel* will be saved"

67. 1 Corinthians 10:18
    "Observe *Israel* after the flesh"

68. 2 Corinthians 3:7
    "the children of *Israel* could not look steadily at the face of Moses"

69. 2 Corinthians 3:13
    "the children of *Israel* could not look steadily at the end"

70. 2 Corinthians 11:22
    "Are they *Israelites*? So am I"

71. Galatians 6:16
    "peace and mercy...upon the *Israel* of God"*

72. Ephesians 2:12
    "aliens from the commonwealth of *Israel*"

---

* This usage restricts the meaning of *Israel* or *Israelite* to only those Israelites who have fulfilled certain spiritual requirements (see chapter 1).

73. Philippians 3:5
    "of the stock of *Israel*"

74. Hebrews 8:8
    "I will make a new covenant with the house of *Israel*"

75. Hebrews 8:10
    "the covenant that I will make with the house of *Israel*" (Heb. 8:8,10; both cited from Jer. 31:31-34)

76. Hebrews 11:22
    "Joseph...made mention of the departure of the children of *Israel*"

77. Revelation 2:14
    "Balaam...put a stumbling block before the children of *Israel*"

78. Revelation 7:4
    "One hundred and forty-four thousand of all the tribes of the children of *Israel*"

79. Revelation 21:12
    "the names of the twelve tribes of the children of *Israel*"

WHEN GOD
GIVES HIS OATH

The following is a list of forty-six passages where God has given His oath concerning the land of Canaan — subsequently renamed the land of Israel. In the New Testament it is this latter name that is used (see Matt. 2:20,21). (Italics have been added.)

In every case, God's commitment is to give this land to Abraham, Isaac, Jacob and their descendants. In three places God's *oath* is joined with His *covenant*, and these passages are marked by a diamond (♦). In three places, also, it is stated explicitly that Israel's possession of the land is to be *forever* or *everlasting*, and these passages are marked by a cross (†).

1. Genesis 24:7
    "The Lord God...*swore* to me [Abraham], saying, 'To your descendants I give this land....' "

2. Genesis 26:3

"...to you [Isaac] and your descendants I give all these lands, and I will perform the *oath* which I *swore* to Abraham your father."

3. Genesis 50:24

"And Joseph said to his brethren... 'God will...bring you out of this land to the land of which He *swore* to Abraham, to Isaac, and to Jacob.' "

4. Exodus 6:8

"And I will bring you [Israel] into the land which I *swore* to give to Abraham, Isaac, and Jacob; and I will give it to you as a heritage: I am the Lord."

5. Exodus 13:5

"And it shall be, when the Lord brings you into the land of the Canaanites and the Hittites and the Amorites and the Hivites and the Jebusites, which He *swore* to your fathers to give you...."

6. Exodus 13:11

"And it shall be, when the Lord brings you into the land of the Canaanites, as He *swore* to you and your fathers, and gives it to you...."

†7. Exodus 32:13

"Remember Abraham, Isaac, and Israel, Your servants, to whom You *swore* by Your own self, and said to them, '...all this land that I have spoken of I give to your descendants, and they shall inherit it *forever.*' "

8. Exodus 33:1
   "Depart and go up from here...to the land of which I *swore* to Abraham, Isaac, and Jacob, saying, 'To your descendants I will give it.' "

9. Numbers 11:12
   "...Carry them in your bosom...to the land which You *swore* to their fathers...."

10. Numbers 14:16
    "...because the Lord was not able to bring this people [Israel] to the land which He *swore* to give them...."

11. Numbers 14:23
    "...they [disbelieving Israelites] certainly shall not see the land of which I *swore* to their fathers, nor shall any of those who rejected Me see it."

12. Numbers 32:11
    "...Surely none of the men who came up from Egypt...shall see the land of which I *swore* to Abraham, Isaac, and Jacob, because they have not wholly followed Me...."

13. Deuteronomy 1:8

   "...go in and possess the land which the Lord *swore* to your fathers — to Abraham, Isaac, and Jacob — to give to them and their descendants after them."

14. Deuteronomy 1:35

   "Surely not one of these men of this evil generation shall see that good land of which I *swore* to give to your fathers...."

15. Deuteronomy 6:10

   "...when the Lord your God brings you into the land of which He *swore* to your fathers, to Abraham, Isaac, and Jacob...."

16. Deuteronomy 6:18

   "...that you may go in and possess the good land of which the Lord *swore* to your fathers...."

17. Deuteronomy 6:23

   "...that He might bring us in, to give us the land of which He *swore* to our fathers."

18. Deuteronomy 7:13

   "And He [God] will love you and bless you and multiply you...in the land of which He *swore* to your fathers to give you."

19. Deuteronomy 8:1

    "...that you may...go in and possess the land of which the Lord *swore* to your fathers."

20. Deuteronomy 9:5

    "It is not because of your righteousness...that you go in to possess their land, but...that He [God] may fulfill the word which the Lord *swore* to your fathers, to Abraham, Isaac, and Jacob."

21. Deuteronomy 10:11

    "Arise, begin your journey before the people, that they may go in and possess the land which I *swore* to their fathers to give them."

22. Deuteronomy 11:9

    "...that you may prolong your days in the land which the Lord *swore* to give your fathers...."

23. Deuteronomy 11:21

    "...that your days and the days of your children may be multiplied in the land of which the Lord *swore* to your fathers to give them...."

24. Deuteronomy 19:8

    "Now if the Lord your God enlarges your territory, as He *swore* to your fathers, and gives you the land which He promised to give to your fathers...."

25. Deuteronomy 26:3
    "...I have come to the country which the Lord *swore* to our fathers to give us."

26. Deuteronomy 26:15
    "...bless Your people Israel and the land which You have given us, just as You *swore* to our fathers...."

27. Deuteronomy 28:11
    "And the Lord will grant you plenty of goods...in the land of which the Lord *swore* to your fathers to give you."

28. Deuteronomy 30:20
    "...that you may dwell in the land which the Lord *swore* to your fathers, to Abraham, Isaac, and Jacob, to give them."

29. Deuteronomy 31:7
    "...you [Joshua] must go with this people to the land which the Lord has *sworn* to their fathers to give them...."

30. Deuteronomy 31:20
    "When I have brought them to the land...of which I *swore* to their fathers."

31. Deuteronomy 31:21
    "...even before I have brought them to the land of which I *swore* to give them."

32. Deuteronomy 31:23

"...you [Joshua] shall bring the children of Israel into the land of which I *swore* to them...."

33. Deuteronomy 34:4

"This is the land of which I *swore* to give Abraham, Isaac, and Jacob, saying, 'I will give it to your descendants.'"

34. Joshua 1:6

"...to this people you [Joshua] shall divide as an inheritance the land which I *swore* to their fathers to give them."

35. Joshua 5:6

"...to whom [disbelieving Israelites] the Lord swore that He would not show them the land which the Lord had *sworn* to their fathers that He would give us...."

36. Joshua 21:43

"So the Lord gave to Israel all the land of which He had *sworn* to give to their fathers...."

♦37. Judges 2:1

"Then the Angel of the Lord...said: 'I...brought you to the land of which I *swore* to your fathers; and I said, "I will never break My *covenant* with you."'"

♦†38. 1 Chronicles 16:15-18
"Remember His *covenant* forever,
The word which He commanded, for a
thousand generations,
The *covenant* which He made with
Abraham,
And His *oath* to Isaac,
And confirmed it to Jacob for a stat-
ute,
To Israel for an *everlasting covenant*,
Saying, 'To you I will give the land of
Canaan....' "

39. Nehemiah 9:15
"You [the Lord]...told them to go in to
possess the land
Which You had *sworn* to give them."

♦†40. Psalm 105:8-11
"He [the Lord] remembers His *cove-
nant* forever,
The word which He commanded, for a
thousand generations,
The covenant which He made with
Abraham,
And His *oath* to Isaac,
And confirmed it to Jacob for a stat-
ute,
To Israel as an *everlasting covenant*,
Saying, 'To you I will give the land of
Canaan....' "

41. Jeremiah 11:5
"...that I may establish the *oath* which
I have *sworn* to your fathers, to give

them 'a land flowing with milk and honey....' "

42. Jeremiah 32:22
"You [the Lord] have given them this land, of which You *swore* to their fathers to give them...."

43. Ezekiel 20:6
"On that day I [the Lord] raised My hand in an *oath* to them, to bring them out of the land of Egypt into a land that I had searched out for them...."

44. Ezekiel 20:28
"When I [the Lord] brought them into the land concerning which I had raised My hand in an *oath* to give them...."

45. Ezekiel 20:42
"Then you shall know that I am the Lord, when I bring you into the land of Israel, into the country for which I raised My hand in an *oath* to give to your fathers."

46. Ezekiel 47:14
"You shall inherit it [the land of Israel] equally with one another; for I raised My hand in an *oath* to give it to your fathers, and this land shall fall to you as your inheritance."

OTHER BOOKS BY DEREK PRINCE

Appointment in Jerusalem
Baptism in the Holy Spirit
Blessing or Curse: You Can Choose
Chords From David's Harp
Christian Foundations Correspondence Course
Does Your Tongue Need Healing?
Extravagant Love
Faith to Live By
Fasting
Fatherhood
Foundation Series (3 volumes)
God Is a Matchmaker
God's Medicine Bottle
God's Plan for Your Money
The Grace of Yielding
The Holy Spirit in You
How to Fast Successfully
If You Want God's Best
In Search of Truth
The Last Word on the Middle East
Life's Bitter Pool
The Marriage Covenant
Objective for Living: To Do God's Will
Pages From My Life's Book
Prayers and Proclamations
Praying for the Government
Rejection: Cause and Cure
Self-Study Bible Course
Shaping History Through Prayer and Fasting
Spiritual Warfare
Thanksgiving, Praise and Worship

For a free catalog of books and materials, contact:
Derek Prince Ministries — International
P.O. Box 300 • Fort Lauderdale, FL 33302-0300
(305) 763-5202

DEREK PRINCE MINISTRIES

Branch Offices

DPM — Australia
2/14 Pembury Road • Minto 2566, New South Wales • Australia

DPM — Canada
P.O. Box 5217 • Halifax, Nova Scotia B3L 4S7 • Canada

DPM — Germany
Urbachstr. 14 • D-7272, Altensteig • Germany

DPM — South Africa
P.O. Box 32406 • Glenstantia 0010 • South Africa

DPM — South Pacific
P.O. Box 2029 • Christchurch 8000 • New Zealand

DPM — United Kingdom
P.O. Box 169 • Enfield, Middlesex EN3 6PL • England

Outreach offices

DPM — China
P.O. Box 269 • York YO1 1FF • England

DPM — Eastern Europe
P.O. Box 234 • 4200 AE Gorinchem • Holland

DPM — Nigeria
P.O. Box 2568 • Ikeja, Lagos • Nigeria